ARTAIR'S TEMPTRESS

HIGHLANDER FATE BOOK FIVE

STELLA KNIGHT

PRONUNCIATION GUIDE

Artair - AHR-tər
Keagan - KEE-gən
Liosa - LEE-oh-SUH
Tamhas - TOM-us
Iomhar - ee-o-VAR
Loirin - LORE-in
Latharn - LA-urn

CHAPTER 1

Present Day
Scottish Highlands

Diana kept her gaze trained on the lush green surroundings of the Scottish Highlands as her Aunt Kensa drove them down a winding road. Kensa hummed softly beneath her breath as she drove, as if this were an ordinary outing, an ordinary task—not a task involving magic. A task involving time travel.

She forced herself to take a calming breath, clenching her hands in her lap. *Deep breaths,* she told herself. *Deep breaths.* But her heart continued to hammer against her chest like a battering ram.

"I know you're nervous," Kensa said, glancing over at her. "But I know you can do this. And I'm so grateful for your help."

"I haven't agreed," Diana swiftly returned,

shooting her aunt a firm look. "Only that I would consider it."

Kensa gave her an amicable nod and continued to hum beneath her breath. Diana recognized the song, an old Gaelic song she used to hear her mother sing.

Kensa was in a disconcertingly good mood, considering the impossible task she'd asked Diana to undertake: traveling back through time. Diana swallowed hard at the very thought. Why was she even considering this?

Her weekend had started with good intentions. She'd come to the Scottish Highlands to work on early renovations of her family's ancestral home, and to enjoy a nice little holiday away from her hectic life as a solicitor in London.

Diana leaned back in her seat, resisting the sudden urge to laugh. If she didn't know all about time travel and witches and magic, she would think her aunt was mad. But she wasn't. Kensa was a stiuireadh, a druid witch who possessed the ability to travel—and to guide other people—through time.

A part of her wished she didn't know about the existence of such things, that she could go about her life as if it didn't exist, like most people. And for the most part she had, turning her back on everything to do with magic and time travel after her parents, who were powerful stiuireadh, died during one of their time-traveling journeys when she was a teenager.

Another aunt had raised her, her Aunt Maggie.

Like Diana, Maggie had no desire to take part in the family business of magic. That was likely because Maggie possessed little magic herself and lived a completely ordinary life as a shopkeeper in a small village in southern England. Maggie had been just fine with Diana turning her back on magic and even encouraged her to do so. It was Kensa who kept trying to lure her back in, Kensa who kept insisting that she needed to embrace who she was—*what* she was.

So, when Kensa had arrived at the manor, uninvited, telling Diana she'd inadvertently sent a man from the past to the present, Diana hadn't been terribly surprised.

The man was Laird Artair Dalaigh, a fourteenth-century Highlander who was now settled in at Kensa's home in an isolated stretch of the Highlands. His descendant, Niall O'Kean, had taken his place in the past, where he was now happily married to Artair's intended, Caitria. Kensa insisted that this was the correct way of things—Niall and Caitria belonged together. She had been the one to influence Niall's dreams using her magic, warning him that Caitria was in danger. Niall had successfully averted the danger, and now he was with his soulmate.

It was Artair who didn't belong in the present. Kensa wanted Diana, who hadn't practiced magic in years, to help guide Artair back to the year he belonged—1390.

"Why can't you do it?" Diana had demanded.

"Time traveling spells are complex. My magic only works on guiding people born in the *present* to the past—since Artair was born in the past, I can't guide him back. I already tried, not long after he arrived—and the spell failed," Kensa said.

"How did this even happen?"

"I'm not sure. But I think that because Niall traveled back in time without a stiuireadh, something went awry—something that sent Artair to this time," Kensa replied with a frustrated sigh.

"Why me? You don't know anyone else who can do it?" Diana asked, desperation sweeping over her.

"There aren't many of us, and the one stiuireadh I know who can perform the necessary spell isn't—well, she isn't available."

"I take it that means she's in another time," Diana muttered, rubbing her temples.

"Yes," Kensa replied, "and I don't know when she's going to return. But you have the magical affinity to perform such a spell, something your parents could do as well—to send someone born in the past back in time."

You haven't agreed to anything, she reminded herself, for the millionth time. She had only agreed to come after Kensa kept pleading with her, on the verge of tears. As frustrating as Diana found her aunt, she loved her—and decided to at least meet this Artair. And she had to admit there was a part of her that was curious—someone from the fourteenth century in this time? What would he be like?

4

"How . . . is he?" she asked hesitantly, as Kensa made a sharp left turn, the car cresting north on a steep incline that angled deeper into the mountains. "This—Highlander."

"He's . . . frustrated. Confused," Kensa said, after a pause. "But most of all, eager to get back to his own time, something I promised I'd help him with."

"Is he angry with Niall O'Kean? That he's taken his place? His bride?"

"No," Kensa said, to her surprise. "When I told him Niall had fallen in love with Caitria and married her, he seemed relieved. I suspect he prefers being alone. Sounds familiar."

Her aunt gave her a sly look, but Diana didn't take the bait. She too preferred her solitude, and there was nothing wrong with that.

They reached the top of the mountain road, and Kensa made a turn onto yet another dirt road that led to what appeared to be a crumbling manor. But Diana knew this was merely a charm to prevent any curious onlookers from coming closer if they even ventured this deep into the Highlands. It was actually a cozy two-story cottage that Kensa had lived in for as long as Diana could remember. Kensa actually had several cottages dotted around the Highlands, using the money from a sizable family inheritance to purchase them. Kensa had told her having the multiple homes helped her assist wayward travelers as they made their way to and from the portal in Tairseach.

Diana had refused to use any of the inheritance after her parents' deaths, though she knew her parents would have wanted her to have it. She simply couldn't bear to touch it after they died; she was happy to make her own money, to live her own life separate from her family's magical legacy.

As they drew closer to Kensa's home, its true form appeared, and as Diana took in its gray steepled roof and red brick façade, a wave of memories swept over her.

She had come here once when she was young to celebrate Yule with her parents and other extended family members, many of whom were stiuireadh. A pang pierced her as one sharp memory entered her mind's eye: standing in a circle with her parents and other family members when she was twelve, including Kensa, as they all sang an ancient druidic hymn. She could remember how happy she felt in that moment, unaware that her parents would be dead the following year.

"It's all right, dear," Kensa said gently, as if reading her thoughts, pulling the car to a stop. She reached out to give Diana's hand a gentle squeeze. "If you help me—and I hope you will—you only need to be here for a night or two."

Diana gave her an abrupt nod and stepped out of the car, forcing herself to push aside her dread—and remnant grief—as she trailed her aunt into the cottage.

She was not prepared for the sight that greeted her when they stepped inside.

A tall man paced in the center of the entry hallway. His clothes were medieval—he wore long dark breeches and a white tunic, partially opened at the throat to reveal a muscular torso beneath. He had wavy chestnut-colored hair that fell to his shoulders, clear blue eyes the color of a summer's sky, proud, aristocratic features, a wide, generous mouth, and a stubble of beard that dotted his square jaw.

He stopped pacing when they entered, turning to face them, his eyes narrowing as they settled on Diana. Her reaction was immediate—and embarrassing. Her face warmed, her mouth went dry, and her heart pounded furiously against her ribcage.

He strode toward her, stopping when he was only inches away. Diana was a tall woman, meeting most men eye to eye, but with Artair, she barely reached his shoulders and had to tilt her head back to meet his stormy blue eyes.

"Is this the lass, Kensa?" he demanded. His voice was a deep rumble, his words heavily accented with a deep Scottish brogue; she had to concentrate to make out each word.

His eyes traveled from the loose shirt she wore beneath her jacket down to her tight yoga pants, his gaze leaving a scorching trail of heat on her skin. Something flared in his eyes, and his mouth tightened. "She looks like a common whore."

Fury chased away her stirrings of desire. She straightened to her full height and returned his glare with a fierce one of her own.

"Excuse me?" she hissed. "I'm here to help you, and the first thing you do is call me a whore?"

"Diana. Artair," Kensa said hastily, moving to stand between them as they glowered at each other. "Now is not the time to trade insults. Artair, I told you before—men and women dress differently in this time. I'm sure you didn't mean it. Do you want to apologize to my niece?"

While Kensa's tone was polite, it was edged with steel. Artair had the decency to look apologetic, taking a step back.

"I apologize, lass," he said gruffly.

"Now, let's try this again, shall we? Diana, this is Laird Artair Dalaigh, though he's fine with being called Artair. Artair, my niece Diana Hartford."

He gave her a jerky nod in greeting, and Diana scowled. He was gorgeous as sin, but rude. She gave him a nod of her own, turning away from him. He'd made her decision very, very easy for her. Her aunt could find someone else to transport this handsome sod through time.

"Can I talk to you alone, Aunt Kensa?" Diana asked tautly.

Kensa blinked in surprise.

"Yes, but I was hoping we could all—"

"I think it's best we talk alone."

Kensa deflated. Her aunt knew her too well: she had to know what she was going to say. But Kensa gave her a polite nod, turning to give Artair a brief smile.

"We'll be back in a moment."

Kensa took Diana to a parlor at the end of the hall, closing the door behind them.

"I won't do it," Diana said, as soon as they were alone. "I'm not the only witch you know. There has to be *someone* else."

"Artair is unnerved by all that's happened. He's usually very considerate," Kensa insisted. "And I'm still working on finding someone else—but taking a person born in the past back to the past is a tricky spell. It's why I need someone like you, someone with a strong affinity for such magic. Diana," she continued, her voice wavering with emotion, "I do what I do to help people. Artair has been torn from his time—he doesn't belong here. The task is simple —you get him to 1390, and then you return to the present. I'll tell him to treat you with nothing but respect going forward."

Diana expelled a sigh, gazing into her aunt's pleading eyes. It was rare to see Kensa, who was often so self-assured, in a state of anxiety.

She closed her eyes. *Just this once,* she told herself. *Just this once, and then you can get back to your normal, nonmagical life.*

"All right," Diana said grudgingly, opening her eyes. "But you'll have to tell me exactly what to do."

CHAPTER 2

*A*rtair resumed his pacing once Kensa and Diana disappeared into the parlor. The woman Kensa had brought with her was not at all who he'd expected. He'd expected an older woman, stooped with age, not the young golden-haired beauty that had stepped into the foyer. A surge of desire filled him at the memory of her—her golden hair, tied back into a bun, her deep brown eyes, a lush mouth that he'd imagined exploring with his own, and firm, taut breasts, the outline of which he could make out beneath the loose tunic she wore. Hips that were delectably curved, which her short, tight breeches emphasized.

The powerful wave of desire that swept over him at the sight of her had disconcerted him; he'd resorted to an insult to pull himself out of his stupor.

He heaved a sigh, closing his eyes. The last

thing he needed was a distractingly lovely lass hovering about, not after all that had occurred.

He could remember every detail of the day he'd been ripped from his own time. He'd made the journey south from his manor with his manservant, Latharn, at his side, ignoring the dread that swirled in his heart. Caitria, the lass he was to marry, was bonnie and kind, but he held no passion for her. He'd agreed to the marriage because it was time for him to wed, and he wanted to make an alliance with the powerful MacGreghor clan. He'd decided it was best he felt no great love or passion for his wife-to-be; he would do his duty and sire a few sons with her and focus on his duties as laird and as a member of his new clan.

He'd just settled into his room at MacGreghor Castle when the room had begun to shake, and he'd wondered if a great horde of horses were approaching the castle. The world had tilted around him, and everything went black.

When he came to, he'd found himself lying sprawled in the center of the ruins of an ancient village.

He'd stood up and looked around, panic and fear racing through his veins.

"Oh no!"

A woman had rushed toward him—Kensa—her eyes wide with alarm. She wore strange clothes and he'd struggled to understand her words, which had come out in a rush. She'd said something about a

Niall O'Kean, switching places, and that he wasn't supposed to be in this time.

As he'd looked down at her in confusion, she'd taken his hands and uttered strange words. When nothing happened, she'd sunk down to her knees, looking up at him in despair.

"I'm so sorry, Artair," she'd said. "I don't know what happened—but you shouldn't be here."

She'd taken him back to a large cottage where over the course of the next few days, she'd tried to explain to him what happened, and it gradually sank in how he'd come to this place.

He'd traveled through time.

A distant descendant of his family, someone who shared his likeness, had taken his place in the past. As soon as this man, this Niall O'Kean, had arrived in his time—Artair had been transported to the present. Artair couldn't believe it when she'd told him the year—over six hundred years beyond his time, in the twenty-first century.

He hadn't believed her at first, of course. He'd thought that perhaps she was a member of a rival clan of the MacGreghors who wanted to stop his wedding to Caitria for some reason, and thought to use trickery to capture him. He'd left the cottage, ignoring her cries of protest, intending to find his way back to the castle, when a giant metal contraption with wheels had nearly run him over. Kensa had helped him back to the cottage, and he'd demanded to know what that thing was.

"That's a car. Something not common until the

twentieth century," she'd said. "I wouldn't lie to you about this, Artair. You're in the twenty-first century."

Only then did he sit with her as she'd explained —or tried to explain—again. She was a stiuireadh, a druid witch who could help travelers through time. She'd told him that Niall had settled into the past where he would stay, and though Caitria and Laird MacGreghor knew he wasn't Artair, he'd found a place there, with Caitria.

He knew the proper response to Niall marrying his intended should be outrage, even jealousy, but he'd only felt relief. Caitria was a good lass who deserved true love and happiness.

He wasn't too worried about his manor or his lands. He had a trusted steward and devoted servants who'd tend to them while he was away. He just wanted to get back to his time . . . to his life.

Kensa stepped into the hallway, pulling him from his thoughts. She raised an eyebrow and placed her hands on her hips, glowering at him as if he were a misbehaving bairn.

"She almost refused to help. You need to treat her with respect, Artair."

"I apologized," he said, scowling.

"I mean it. If you want to get back to your own time . . ."

"I ken," he said, giving her a firm nod. "I'll apologize tae the lass again."

Kensa looked satisfied by this and moved past him to look out of the side windows that framed the front door. He'd become familiar with Kensa during the past few weeks, and he'd come to like her, though he was initially angry that the magic she'd performed had inadvertently sent him here.

Magic. The word most commonly used in his time was witchcraft. He'd always been a sensible man, not prone to the superstitions of those around him, but he couldn't deny that he was indeed in another time, especially after he'd seen the metal beast that Kensa called a car. How else could he have arrived in another time if not by witchcraft?

Those in his time associated witchcraft with evil, but he could detect no trace of evil or wickedness with Kensa—he was good at gleaning people's characters, and he only saw goodness in the woman.

She'd kept him at the cottage, bringing him food and drink, insisting that he shouldn't attempt to venture out while she sought another stiuireadh who could bring him back to his own time.

"It'll overwhelm you if you venture far," she'd insisted. "Things are—faster in this time. Louder. It'll serve no purpose, especially considering you don't belong here."

And though he was curious about this future world that existed beyond these walls, he'd obliged, only leaving to take brief walks around the cottage. He'd realized the cottage must be nestled deep within the Highlands; nothing but nature—sprawling glens and rolling mountains shrouded in mist—surrounded it. The only obvious difference between his time and this future time were the paved snake-like roads and the occasional metal beast that roared past. He could almost pretend he was in his own time, enjoying the solitude of his manor.

"You need to give my niece some time," Kensa was saying now. "She has powerful time-travel magic in her bloodline, but she's turned her back on it for most of her life. She believes that such magic killed her parents, so this is all difficult for her."

"I will," he promised, shame twisting his gut as he recalled his harsh words to Diana.

Kensa smiled, reaching out to give his hand a brief squeeze.

"I'll prepare lunch, then we can all talk."

WHEN HE ENTERED the dining room later, Kensa had already set out a meal of stew and fresh bread. Diana was already there, her back to him as she stared out one of the windows. He noticed she'd changed into a pair of dark blue breeches and a short-sleeved tunic that Kensa had told him was called a "T-shirt" in this time. The clothing was slightly less scandalous than what she'd worn when he first met her, but they still clung to every one of her lush curves. He swallowed, forcing himself to push aside the desire that flared inside him. This woman was a witch who could help him transport through time, not a lass to lust after.

"Diana," he said.

She turned, her eyes widening briefly at the sight of him. She gave him a curt nod.

"Artair," she returned, her tone cool.

"I wanted tae apologize again—tae truly apologize—for my harsh words earlier," he said, stepping forward. "I believe in treating lasses with the utmost respect, and ye deserve mine."

Her expression softened, and she gave him a cautious smile, one that made her features even more lovely; it was like watching a flame roar to life after being snuffed out.

"Thank you," she said. "I—I'm sorry for your circumstances. My magic is a little rusty, but I'll try my best to get you back to your time."

He nodded his thanks, trying to come up with more words to say, but he was inexplicably nervous around her. Fortunately, he didn't need to say more, as Kensa entered with a tray of tea.

"I see you two have made amends," she said, beaming. "Let's eat and discuss, shall we?"

"I'm going to spend the rest of the day—and tomorrow—working with Diana on the spell she'll need to perform to get you back to your time," Kensa said, when they'd all taken their seats. "If all goes well, she'll get you back to 1390 and then return to this time. Artair," Kensa continued, turning to face him, "when you get back—"

"I ken," he interjected. "Donnae tell anyone where I've truly been—except for those I trust the most."

It was something they'd discussed in detail. Few people knew of time travel or of the stiuireadh; such knowledge would only cause fear and chaos. Besides, Artair had no intention of telling people in his time that he'd traveled to the twenty-first century. They would think he was mad. He and Kensa had worked out a story that explained where he'd been. He would tell Latharn and the others that he'd left the castle to go riding, but he'd fallen from his horse and slipped into unconsciousness. A local healer had taken him in and tended to him during the weeks he was in his false sleep—Kensa told him the modern-day term was "coma"—until he was well again and made his way back home.

"I have attire for Diana to wear when she travels with you. And I'm going to give you both plenty of coin to take with you. Diana, you'll have to use a special spell to take the money back in time with you—travelers usually can't take extra physical objects with them to the past."

"Why do I need money?" Diana asked, paling slightly. "I thought you said this would be a quick trip—as soon as I get Artair to his time, I'll return."

"It's just a precaution," Kensa said gently. "Things can go wrong with time travel. I hope that you won't need to use it."

He could see the hesitation on Diana's lovely face, and something compelled him to lean forward.

"I may not be able tae perform witchcraft," he said, meeting Diana's gaze and holding it. "But I'll keep ye safe if something goes awry. Ye have my word."

Their gaze held for several moments. As her brown eyes locked with his, a flare of awareness stirred within him. She finally gave him a nod and averted her gaze.

"Let's hope you don't have to," she said, with a smile that seemed forced.

For the rest of the meal, Kensa told Diana that they'd spend the next two days practicing her magic, and then he and Diana could depart. He noticed that Diana remained tense; at the end of the meal she politely excused herself and scurried from the room. Kensa watched her go, concern marring her features.

"This is so hard for her," Kensa said, with a heavy sigh. "I hate to get her involved, but we have to get you back soon. You've been here for too long."

A fissure of alarm wound through him.

"What do ye mean?"

She hesitated a moment before responding.

"I can . . . sense when someone belongs in a particular time. The people I've helped travel—they often belong in a different time, with their soul mate. But when someone travels to a time in which they don't belong and lingers for too long—it's hard to explain, but *time* doesn't like it. Wayward travelers who linger too long in a time they don't belong have taken ill or simply disappeared."

He stared at her, his heart hammering—her

words had thoroughly chilled him. She reached out to give his hand a reassuring squeeze.

"I didn't mean for my words to alarm you. You'd have to be here much longer for any ill effects to take hold—but it's best to get you back soon just in case. Diana may be unsure of her abilities, but I'm confident my niece can get you back to where you belong."

CHAPTER 3

"*T*ry again," Kensa urged.

Diana gritted her teeth in frustration, pushing away the grimoire.

It was early the next morning, and after she'd informed her assistant and her bosses by email that she'd be extending her holiday, she'd spent three useless hours reviewing basic magical spells in Kensa's cramped study—none of which she'd been able to master. She had exactly two days to reacquaint herself with magic she hadn't used in years. She knew that two days wasn't enough time, but Kensa was adamant about getting Artair back sooner rather than later.

"I'm no good at this," Diana said, rubbing her temples. "At this rate, I'll transport myself and Artair to the distant future—and kill us both in the process."

"Tairseach is a portal; the magic for time travel

is already there. As a stiuireadh, you have the ability to manipulate it."

"If I have such an affinity for time travel, for magic—then why can't I perform any of these basic spells?" Diana demanded, gesturing toward the grimoire.

"You haven't performed magic for some time. But it will come to you; it's already in you," Kensa insisted. "You just have to keep trying."

Diana briefly considered telling her aunt that no, she couldn't do this, and she was already tired of trying. But the desperation—and faith—on her aunt's face stayed her tongue.

"All right," Diana said, heaving a sigh. "I'll try again."

She looked down at the grimoire Kensa had given her—a grimoire passed down through all the stiuireadh of their family. "Time-weaving" spells filled its pages—spells to assist stiuireadh through time, and guide others, along with defensive and offensive spells. Kensa had tried to explain how it all worked—that time travel already existed, the flow of time wasn't in a straight line as most people thought, and that all the stiuireadh did was help guide others through time's meandering streams using their magic.

But it all still seemed so baffling to Diana. To travel to a different time—or to help another person travel through time—involved complex spells, most of which were in Gaelic, some in Latin, others in Scots and modern English.

Practicing magic was a far cry from her job as a solicitor who dealt with property laws on a daily basis—property law could be complex, but at least it made sense.

Still, she gritted her teeth and straightened her shoulders.

"All right," she muttered. "Let's try again."

Diana practiced several basic spells, which included opening and closing the door with a simple gesture of her hand and a silent command in Gaelic, along with a Levitation spell, during which she lifted the grimoire from the desk using only her magic. She had to admit that she felt a rush of delight at the sensation of her magic beneath her skin—like a gust of wind rippling through her, or a jolt of electricity.

"See? You're already improving," Kensa said, beaming.

"These are just basic spells. What if I can't get Artair back?"

"You will. I have absolute faith in you, niece. You have to rid yourself of that self-doubt. Our magic is within us and connects with our emotions. You can do this. But for now," she said, standing and placing her hand on Diana's shoulder. "I think you should take a break. We've been in here for hours."

Diana turned to glance out of the window, her eyes widening with surprise. It was already getting dark—they'd now spent most of the day in Kensa's study practicing.

Kensa led her to the dining room where Artair was already waiting for them. She hadn't seen him all day, other than a brief glimpse of him taking a walk around the grounds as she'd practiced a Silencing spell by the window—and she'd quickly averted her eyes at the sight of him. She found him . . . disarming.

He met her eyes, giving her a warm smile, and her heart performed a small catapult in her chest. She returned his smile and looked away; she couldn't let his attractiveness distract her, not when she needed to concentrate on the monumental task of guiding him back through time.

"Diana's doing well with her magic," Kensa said cheerfully to Artair, as she set down bowls of lamb stew, which had been on the stove all day.

Diana gave her aunt a look at the compliment— Kensa was exaggerating. She'd gotten better at what little she knew, but she was far from "doing well." She said nothing, opting not to dispute Kensa's words, and concentrated on eating the savory stew, her stomach letting out a satisfied grumble—one she hoped Artair didn't hear.

"I think you can help Diana as well, Artair," Kensa continued. "Before you retire for the night, you can tell Diana about several things that remind you of your time. Imagery is a powerful thing with magic, it'll make her spell more potent."

Diana looked up; Artair was nodding in agree- ment, and anxiety swirled through her gut. She knew her aunt was right, that such imagery would be helpful, but how could she focus on whatever he told her when he disarmed her so much?

"I think that's a fine idea," Artair said. "I'll gladly help."

Diana took a sip of wine and nodded. *Just focus,* she urged herself. She'd been around handsome men before, had dated handsome men—though none affected her the way Artair did, and she'd known him for all of five minutes.

Kensa left them alone shortly after, telling them she needed to check on something, but Diana suspected she was leaving them alone on purpose.

"Shall I tell ye now, lass?" Artair asked, his blue eyes meeting hers. "I see no reason tae wait."

"Yes," she said, setting down her wine. *Focus.* "Just three things will suffice. Preferably memories that affect your senses—sight, sound, taste, touch."

"Ah," he said, settling back in his chair, raking his hand through his chestnut hair. She noticed that he wore his dark tunic slightly open at the throat, and she could again glimpse his muscular torso beneath. A shard of heat pierced her; she had to force herself to look at his face. "There's my manor. 'Tis been in my family for generations."

Diana noticed that there was no emotion behind his words; he might as well have been reciting a recipe.

"Is there something specific about it?" she asked. "Some place—a room, a garden—that brings you comfort?"

He looked startled for a moment before his

expression changed. Now she saw a longing in his eyes.

"There's a grove, tucked away not far from my manor. My grandfather told me that the druids who used tae dwell in our lands held rituals there. I suppose that's why there's something . . . magical about the place. I go there when I need time tae myself; I went there after my father died and my sister left the manor. 'Tis always brought me great comfort. It smells of damp earth, honeysuckle and fallen leaves."

Diana tried to remain clinical as he spoke, to file away his words to memory so she could easily recall them when she performed her spell. But there was something about the way his eyes lit up as he spoke that filled her with warmth.

"Good," she said. "That helps. Is there anything else? A person, perhaps?"

She thought of Caitria, the woman he was supposed to marry, who had married Niall O'Kean instead. Though Kensa had told her Artair had expressed relief at the news, a sudden tension seized her as she waited for his response.

"Aye," he said, and her stomach tightened, as he continued, "my sister."

The tension in Diana's stomach dissipated when she realized he wasn't speaking of Caitria—though that was foolish. It shouldn't matter if he did pine over her his ex-fiancée; she barely knew the man.

"I didn't know you had a sister," Diana said.

A shadow fell over his face. "We've not spoken for many years. 'Tis a long tale, but we didnae part well. She lives near the border of Scotland with her husband, whom I've never met. I imagine she doesnae even ken I'm gone—and if she does, I donnae think she cares."

"You don't know that," she said gently.

A long pause stretched as Artair looked past her, his eyes far away. When his gaze returned to hers, it was guarded, as if a window had firmly shut.

"Do ye need anything more?" he asked shortly.

"No," she said, though she was curious for more details about his sister. But by the shuttered expression on his face, she could tell he didn't want to divulge any more personal information. "I think I have enough."

She stood. Artair stood as well, moving around the table to stand close to her. Heat spiraled through her as he reached down to take her hand; awareness flaring to life beneath her skin at his touch.

"I just wanted tae thank ye," he murmured. "For doing this. Yer aunt told me 'tis not easy for ye —after what happened tae yer kin."

Now Diana's guard rose, annoyance prickling her. She didn't want Kensa telling strangers about the tragedy of her past. Her few friends back in London didn't even know the true nature of her parents' deaths—not that they'd believe her if she told them.

"It's—no problem," she said, stepping back from him. "I'll see you tomorrow."

She hurried out of the kitchen, her skin still pulsating from his touch. It wasn't her magic that was the most difficult to grapple with—it was her growing attraction to Artair.

DIANA DREW her cloak around her, the brisk, cold air of the morning piercing her skin like the tip of a knife's blade. It was just past dawn, and she stood with Kensa and Artair just outside the cottage. She wore a fourteenth-century outfit, of which Kensa had many—a forest-green wool cloak, a light underdress and tunic that she wore under a gown of deep blue. Kensa had insisted that she looked lovely, but Diana felt silly and out of place in the gown. Artair, however, looked every inch the fourteenth-century Highland laird, with a white tunic, a pair of breeches, and a wool cloak of his own. His chestnut hair was windswept, his cerulean eyes a bright blue in the early morning sunlight. It took great effort not to stare at him. *Focus.*

"Are you ready?" Kensa asked them, but Diana knew the question was mostly directed at her.

Three days had passed since she'd arrived at the cottage with Kensa. The day before she'd spent the entire day learning Time-weaving spells. She'd barely seen Artair yesterday, and she'd wondered if he was avoiding her after telling her that personal story about his sister.

Diana felt as if they'd barely scratched the surface of the spells, but Kensa assured her that such magic was mostly instinctive, that the portal of Tairseach would do most of the heavy lifting when it came to traveling back through time.

"You just say the words and focus, and it'll guide you to where you need to go," Kensa had assured her.

Now, Diana gave her aunt a nod, though she was still uncertain if she was ready for this. Kensa was using magic to transport them to Tairseach; it was faster, and she wanted them, especially Diana, to get used to magical means of transport.

Kensa took both of their hands and closed her eyes, murmuring the words of a spell in Gaelic.

"Gabh sinn gu Tairseach."

Diana felt a tug of wind on her body, and a spiraling darkness filled her vision. When she opened her eyes, she stood on the outskirts of the ruins of Tairseach.

Artair stumbled back, taking a deep breath.

"I donnae think I'll get used tae that mode of transport," he said, shaking his head in amazement as he looked around.

Diana stepped forward, her gaze trained on the ruins of Tairseach. How many times had she come here as a child while her parents performed rituals with the other stiuireadh? How many times had she giggled and played among the old, crumbling buildings with the other children until her parents found her, playfully scolding her as they swung her up into their arms?

"Diana?"

Diana turned. She hadn't realized that she still lingered on the outskirts of the village while Artair and Kensa had already stepped forward. She mentally shook off the vestiges of nostalgia and approached them.

"This is where I leave you," Kensa said, stepping forward to embrace Artair, before turning to embrace her. "You're stronger than you realize," she whispered in Diana's ear, giving her hand a squeeze.

And before Diana could reply—or ask her to stay to make sure she performed the spell right—Kensa vanished. Diana frowned at the empty space where her aunt had just stood; she had done that on purpose. The message was clear: it was time to use her own magic.

She turned to face Artair, who looked at her with calm expectation. It struck her then that this man had put his life in her hands. She couldn't let him down. She wouldn't. She took a deep breath, approaching him. *You can do this,* she thought to herself.

"Take my hands," she said.

He obeyed, slipping his hands into hers, and a sense of calm settled over her. A sense of . . . rightness. She closed her eyes, reveling in the sensation, and whispered the words of a Time-weaving spell, words she'd practiced repeatedly the day and night before.

"*Snàthain ùine, cluinn m 'ghairm. Snàithnean tìde, cluinn m'anam. Stiùireadh a thoirt dhuinn sàbhailte tro do shlighe chun an ama a dh'fhalbh.*"

As she murmured the words, she drew on Artair's memories. She imagined the grove he'd told her about in her mind's eye—leaves dappled with sunlight, the scent of damp earth. She thought of the pain and emotion in Artair's voice as he spoke of his sister.

Soon, she felt the wind pick up around them. Diana held tight onto Artair's hands, continuing to repeat the words of the spell, and as she opened her eyes to meet Artair's—the modern-day world vanished around them.

CHAPTER 4

Unknown Time
Unknown Place

When the world faded up around them, Artair lay sprawled on the ground. Somehow, Diana had ended up on top of him, her breathing rapid, her heart thundering in tandem with his. She opened her eyes, her lovely brown eyes locking with his, and time seemed suspended for a moment as they gazed at each other.

And then she seemed to realize where she was, hastily rolling off of him, her face flaming. He stumbled to his feet, looking around as he forced himself to quell his arousal—which had grown at the feel of her body against his.

Awe spiraled through him as he looked around. Had Diana's spell truly drawn them through time?

They stood in the center of a wide, open glen,

covered in a light frost. A thick patch of trees dotted the horizon. The sun was setting just beyond it, casting the sky above in an array of colors —deep orange, pink and lavender.

He realized with a sinking dread that he didn't recognize their surroundings; he knew every detail of the lands that surrounded his manor. They could be anywhere.

"This isn't it, is it?" Diana asked, as if reading his thoughts, her voice shaky with apprehension. "I knew I would fail at this. I'm so sorry, Artair."

"There's no need tae apologize, lass," he said, trying to feign a calmness he didn't feel as he faced her with a gentle smile. "We'll just have tae figure out exactly where—and when—we are."

He was grateful that Kensa had insisted on placing coins into hidden pockets in their clothing, money they could use to travel in case they ended up in the wrong place. He'd widened his eyes at the amount she'd given them. When he'd asked how she'd gotten so much coin, Kensa had merely given him a mysterious smile.

"Is it just me," Diana said, pulling him back to the present. "Or is it colder in this time—whenever we are?"

He studied her, noticing that besides her paleness, she was shivering. It was bitterly cold, and that wool cloak wouldn't be enough to keep her warm. He reached out to draw her into the circle of his arms. At his action, she looked at him with surprise.

"Ye need tae keep warm," he said, keeping his tone even, though her nearness had reawakened his arousal. "Let's walk."

He picked a direction—north, from the direction the sun was setting—and they began to walk. They'd only made it a few steps when he heard the approaching thunder of horse hooves.

"Stay behind me," he said, moving to stand before her, his eyes trained on a patch of trees to the north, where several men on horseback raced toward them.

"Try tae avoid speaking if you can," he told Diana. "If we're in the past, yer way of speech will only cause suspicion."

Diana swallowed, but nodded her head in agreement.

As the men drew near, he took in their clothing, and a small fissure of relief filled him. They wore tunics and breeches similar to his own—they must be in the right time, or at least close to it. But wariness replaced his relief as he took in the looks of suspicion and restrained hostility on the men's faces.

There were a half dozen of them. They all looked to be around his age, their strong bodies apparent even from atop their horses. These men weren't mere farmers or peasants. These were men accustomed to fighting. His body tensed as he noticed the way one of them, a burly red-haired man, studied Diana—with a hunger he didn't attempt to hide. Artair straightened to his full height, a surge of fierce protectiveness roiling through him.

"What brings ye tae our lands?" asked a tall dark-haired man with a ragged scar that slashed down his left cheek, giving him an air of danger.

Artair's heart sank. The man didn't speak with the Highland brogue he knew well; it was pure lowland Scots. He'd heard this same accent when he'd traveled along the border of Scotland. His chest tightened as he realized that could be where they were—the conflict-riddled Scottish border.

"We were traveling, and bandits robbed our traveling coach. We've lost our way," he said evenly.

He noticed with dread that the red-haired man continued to stare at Diana. Though she stood behind him, he sensed her unease. He moved to block Diana from the man's view, giving him a challenging glare.

"Where are the other travelers?" the first man who'd addressed him demanded.

"Scattered. We havenae seen them since the robbery. We were going tae make our way on foot tae the nearest village tae arrange for further transport," he said, pleased with himself for his spontaneous lie. But he just wanted to get these men away from Diana. He ached for his sword—for any weapon. "Can ye direct us tae it?"

The men exchanged a glance, a silent understanding seeming to pass between them. Artair braced himself. If necessary, he could tell Diana to run—or perform a spell to get herself out of here—while he tried to fight them off.

He waited in tense silence. Finally, the dark-haired man, whom Artair assumed was their leader, spoke.

"It wouldnae be hospitable for us tae allow ye tae travel on foot in this cold. It looks like it will snow. We can take ye tae the nearest village; my brother and I run an inn there. Then we can see about getting ye horses. I'm called Tamhas," he continued, and pointed to the red-haired man, who continued to stare at Diana. "And this is my brother Iomhar."

Tamhas introduced the rest of the men, who did not nod or give them any sort of greeting. Artair hesitated, his instincts for danger on fire, wanting to refuse and chance their way on foot. But he had a feeling Tamhas wouldn't take no for an answer—and that would increase the already thick tension between them. He turned to Diana, who looked pale and shaken.

"'Tis all right," he whispered, reaching out to grip her hand. "I'll make sure ye donnae come tae any harm."

She swallowed and gave him a jerky nod, not taking her eyes off of the men.

"Very well," Artair said, addressing Tamhas. "I thank ye for yer kindness."

Iomhar dismounted from his horse, practically licking his lips as he approached Diana.

"I'll ride with the lass," he said.

Acting on pure instinct, Artair tucked Diana closer to his side.

"I'll ride with ye," he said, giving him a challenging glare. "My wife will ride with another one of yer men."

He didn't know where this lie came from, but he knew Diana would be safest if they thought she was his wife, and therefore under his protection. He prayed that Diana went along with his lie. To his relief, she remained silent.

Iomhar's face tightened. He turned to look at Tamhas, who gave him a subtle shake of his head. Iomhar returned Artair's glare but turned back to his horse without another word.

Artair climbed onto Iomhar's horse, trying not to react to his pungent smell of old ale. He glanced over at Tamhas, watching as he helped Diana onto his horse. Tamhas treated Diana respectfully, not touching her longer than necessary. Still, he could see that Diana was shaking, and a rush of sympathy coursed through him. The lovely lass had transported him through time for his sake. He would make certain she got safely back to her own time. As soon as they were alone, he would insist that she perform whatever witchcraft she needed to get herself home.

As they rode, Artair eyed his surroundings. It was growing dark and nothing looked familiar.

The ride was brief, with the large glen leading to a dirt road that took them to a small village. They rode until they arrived at an inn, dismounting as two stable boys hurried forward to take their horses.

As soon as they all dismounted, he hurried to Diana, taking her hand. She met his eyes as if to ask, *What do we do now?* He hoped she could read his answer in his eyes: *Just trust me.*

Keeping her hand in his, he followed the men into the bustling inn. Dread pooled in his stomach at the sight of even more men inside, sitting at various long tables, stuffing themselves with bread and ale.

"Loirin, ale and bread for our guests," Tamhas said, addressing a dark-haired woman who was pouring ale to several male patrons.

Tamhas took a seat at one of the few empty tables and gestured for Artair and Diana to sit. Artair felt every male eye in the room on them—on Diana—and he wanted to refuse, to ask Tamhas to just take them to their room. But again, he had the feeling they had no choice.

He took a seat next to Diana, making certain to put an arm over the back of her chair as Iomhar trained his lecherous gaze on her. Loirin approached, keeping her gaze low, and he noticed that her hands were trembling. He wondered why she was so terrified. Were these men keeping her prisoner?

"This is our sister, Loirin," Tamhas said, as if reading his mind. "I donnae ken why she feels the need tae act like a frightened mouse around her kin."

Loirin said nothing in response, only giving them a brief nod of acknowledgment before scurrying away.

"I'd recognize the Highland accent anywhere," Tamhas continued, studying Artair intently. "What are ye called? And what's a Highlander doing this far south?"

"I'm called Domnall," he lied. It was best they didn't know his real name—or that he was a wealthy Highland laird. He wasn't known in the Lowlands, but they could send a spy to the Highlands and inquire about him if they knew his name. "This is my wife, Ilsa. My wife and I were visiting her family in England," he said, emphasizing the word "wife." "We made our way just over the border when those damned bandits set upon us— stole our horses and our belongings."

Tamhas just stared at him, his expression unreadable; Artair couldn't tell if he believed his story or not. Iomhar, however, scowled at him, and again turned his focus to Diana.

"How did such a bonnie Sassenach such as yerself end up married to this beast of a Highlander?"

Artair could tell his words were supposed to be said in jest, but there was a harshness to his tone, and Diana tensed at his side.

"I married the man I love," Diana said simply.

As he feared, both men stiffened at her accent. Tamhas's eyes narrowed, but he remained silent.

"'Tis an odd accent ye have, lass, and I've heard

men from France speak," Iomhar said, prompting laughter from the men at the adjoining table who were openly following their conversation. "What part of England are ye from?"

"A small village in the south," Diana said. Her hand trembled on his leg; she wasn't prepared for such questions. He needed to get them out of here.

"We thank ye for the food," Artair said, setting down his ale and getting to his feet. He hoped that his smile and tone was light though his heart pounded so furiously he feared they could hear it. "But my wife and I are weary from our journey."

"Ye've only just arrived," Tamhas said, with a smile that didn't reach his dark eyes. "Why donnae ye stay for another round of ale?"

Artair's chest tightened. Again, he suspected this wasn't a request.

"Well, I'm not one tae turn down more ale," he said, forcing false cheer into his tone. "But my wife needs her rest."

Tamhas studied him. The silence crackled with tension. Artair was very aware of every eye on them, watching the exchange with interest.

"Clear out," Tamhas announced to the other men in the room. "We wish tae speak tae our guests alone."

Hot panic consumed his entire body. He cursed himself; he should have refused to come here. He turned to Diana, who had gone pale, keeping his voice low.

"Get out of here," he hissed, as the men cleared

41

out—all except for Iomhar and two large men, he noted with unease. "I donnae care if they see ye vanish—leave now."

"I won't leave you," Diana said, looking at him with wide, panicked eyes. "We'll *both* leave."

"Neither of ye are going anywhere," Tamhas said.

Artair faced Tamhas, moving to stand in front of Diana. Tamhas was smiling, but there was no trace of amusement in the smile.

"Not until ye tell me who ye really are."

"I donnae ken what ye—" Artair began.

"There's no clear road where we found ye— especially if ye were crossing the border into Scotland," Tamhas said calmly. "Truth be told, the only bandits who roam these parts are me and my men. And ye and yer wife have been on edge since ye entered the tavern. If this is even yer wife."

"Of course she's my wife," Artair snapped, but Tamhas clearly didn't believe him, his eyes narrowing.

He stood, and Artair sized him up. They were the same height and build, but Tamhas had the benefit of numbers on his side.

"Step aside," Tamhas said coolly. "I wish tae address yer "wife."

Artair gave him a mirthless smile of his own.

"Ye'll not speak tae my wife. We'll leave, and ye and yer men willnae follow," Artair returned.

Iomhar and the other men stood, their hands going to the hilts of their swords.

"I tried tae be friendly," Tamhas said with a sigh. He turned to his men with a bored gesture. "Take them. I want tae question them separately."

Fury paired with panic roiled through him as one of the men moved toward Diana, and she let out a startled, frightened cry. Artair lunged toward him, but someone struck him from behind, and his world dissolved to black.

CHAPTER 5

I knew I couldn't do this, Diana silently railed at herself as she paced the small room that one of the men had thrown her into, her heart in her throat. Not only had she transported them to the wrong place—she'd landed them right into danger. She should have refused Kensa's request and insisted that she find someone else.

If those men hurt—or killed—Artair . . .

Anguish twisted her gut, and she closed her eyes, trying to quell her panic with several steadying breaths.

After one of the men had knocked Artair out, another had approached her, grabbing her arm and leading her up the stairs and into this room, where he'd locked her in. She could hear his breathing outside the door; he was standing guard.

She leaned back against the wall, pressing her fingers to her temples. She had briefly—but only briefly—considered doing what Artair had told her to do, to perform a spell and get the hell out of this time period. But she couldn't leave him behind with those men.

Think. As a solicitor, she was used to solving complex problems, but those problems didn't involve dangerous men from a different time period. She needed to rescue Artair and get them both out of here—to somewhere she could safely perform a Transport spell. *If I can even manage that,* she thought, with a surge of frustration. What if she ended up transporting them to somewhere far more dangerous? But with the way things were going, she didn't have a choice.

She didn't know what they were doing to Artair at the moment, but she had no doubt in her mind as to the intentions of Iomhar—the creepy sod had done nothing but leer at her. Her skin crawled at the thought of him touching her, and a hard resolve settled in. She wouldn't let him come near her.

Diana whirled as the door swung open and Tamhas entered. She swallowed and took a faltering step back.

"There's no need tae be frightened of me, lass."

"Isn't there?" Diana returned, raising her eyebrows. "You've taken me and my husband hostage."

"I just need tae ask ye some questions."

"We mean you no harm," Diana insisted. "You were the ones who found us. We just want to be on our way."

"But that's what we're struggling with, my

lady," he said. "How is it ye ended up where ye did?"

"We told you," she said. "We lost our way—"

"Which is a lie," he said with a sigh, raking his hand through his hair. "Just tell me the truth, lass, and I'll let ye go."

We traveled through time from the twenty-first century.

"I told you," she repeated, hoping that she sounded truthful enough. She met his gaze and held it, something she did whenever she was trying to gain a client's trust during a case. "We are telling you the truth."

He studied her for a long time, as if trying to ascertain the truth of her words. She kept her gaze steady, praying that she was convincing him.

"Yer husband said something odd earlier. He said, 'I donnae care if they see ye vanish.' What did he mean by that?"

Diana froze, her mouth going dry. Why did he have to be so bloody perceptive? And why did Artair have to say that in front of Tamhas?

"He just wanted me to run," she said, hoping that she sounded calmer than she felt. "I—I keep telling you nothing but the truth."

"No, ye're not, lass." He took a step toward her, and she took another step back. He stopped, holding up his hands to show her he meant no harm. "Will ye tell me one thing that's true? Is Domnall yer husband?"

She blinked at the name 'Domnall' before

remembering it was the false name Artair have given him. She thought of Artair, his warm blue eyes as he silently urged her to trust him, how he'd tried to protect her from these men, even though he barely knew her, and the awareness that coursed through her whenever he was near.

"Yes," she said, and his expression softened. "He's my husband. He means more to me than anyone."

"Finally, the truth," he said, giving her a nod of satisfaction, and surprise roiled through her— surprise she had to hide. Maybe there was some benefit to her attraction to Artair after all.

"Please," she implored him. "Don't harm my husband. We just want to be on our way."

"Yer husband is alive and well in the cellar. We have no intention of harming him, lass—as long as he tells us the truth."

He turned and strode out of the room, shutting the door behind him, and she heard the lock turn. She sank down onto the narrow bed, shaking.

Think.

"Magic is the flow of our need, what we truly want," her mother had once told her, as she performed a Levitation spell on a grimoire while a young Diana watched in awe. "All you have to do is direct it where to go—and what to do. It's a part of you. Remember that, love."

Diana stilled, her heart picking up its pace. She thought of Iomhar, his leering gaze.

And she knew exactly what to do.

She moved to the door and called for the guard. He opened the door, glaring at her.

"I'd like to speak with Iomhar."

IOMHAR ENTERED MOMENTS LATER; she heard him order the guard to leave before stepping inside the room. She took a breath as she faced him, setting aside the disgust that filled her stomach when his eyes raked over her with a sickening thoroughness.

"Greetings, my lady," he said, giving her an exaggerated bow. "Ye wished tae speak tae me?"

You're doing this for the greater good, she told herself. She licked her dry lips and stepped forward, giving him what she hoped was a seductive smile.

"I want to offer you a deal."

He raised his eyebrow, his eyes dropping down to her breasts. "A deal, aye?"

"Yes," she said, lowering her eyes to hide her revulsion. "If you agree to let us go, I'll show you my gratitude."

He straightened, pleasure filling his eyes, along with a slight trace of suspicion.

"And why would ye do that, lass?"

"I see the way you've been looking at me," she said, hoping her voice was light, playful, even though she had to force each word past her lips.

"Things have been . . . difficult between Domnall and I."

"Aye?" he asked, stepping forward. It took everything in her power not to step back.

"Yes," she murmured. "But you have to agree to let us go. Perhaps I won't even want to leave . . . after."

His smile widened, and he stepped closer to her, reaching out to touch her cheek. He reeked of sweat and old ale. She forced a smile and reached up to grab his hand before he could touch her.

"Do I have your word?"

"I donnae have tae guarantee ye anything, lass. I could just take what I want," he growled. A jolt of fear struck her, but his expression relaxed. "Yet it will be more pleasurable for us both if ye're not struggling. I'll talk tae my brother about freeing ye. Tell him ye're telling the truth. But only after ye please me."

"Of course," she said, keeping the smile pinned on her face, ignoring the bile that rose in her throat.

"No more talk. I want tae taste ye," he grunted, reaching out to grab her by the nape of her neck.

She acted fast, training her eyes on his, putting every ounce of her fury into the spell.

"*Codladh anois, codladh domhain.*"

It worked. All too well.

The bastard immediately lost consciousness, and she took great pleasure in seeing the brief moment of panicked fear in his eyes before they shut. She hurried forward before he could crash to the floor and create a noise that would surely alert the others.

She caught his bulk in her arms and lowered him to the floor, glowering at him. She had a feeling she wasn't the only woman he would have forced his attentions upon. Kensa had taught her a spell that could cause death in the direst of circumstances, but she'd cautioned Diana to only use it if her life—or someone else's—was in mortal peril. And as much as she loathed the man, she didn't think she could live with his death on her conscience. If her spell held, he'd sleep soundly for the rest of the night—and the next day—before waking.

She reached down and took his dagger from his sword belt, expelling a breath. This wasn't the hardest part of her plan. Artair was in the cellar—she had to get to him.

She slipped open the door, peeking out. The hallway was empty, and relief swept over her that Iomhar had sent her guard away. She heard no noise; given how long they had imprisoned her in the room, it should be the middle of the night. The inn was still and quiet.

She crept down the hall, praying that the guard was nowhere nearby. But all remained silent, and she made her way down the stairs, hurrying across the main room of the inn to reach a second set of stairs, which led down to a dark cellar.

She found Artair there, tied up next to a sack of

barley, and the relief that coursed through her was so great she swayed on her feet.

He turned toward her and she saw that he sported a bruised jaw, along with a swollen left eye. Anger coursed through her; she should have done more damage to Iomhar.

"Diana?" he whispered, paling at the sight of her. "I told ye tae leave."

"And I told you," she returned firmly, kneeling down to undo his binds, "I'm not leaving you behind."

"How did ye get down here?"

"I'll tell you later. We need to go."

He nodded, and she handed him the dagger she'd taken off of Iomhar. Together they made their way back up to the main room.

As soon as they emerged, Diana froze. Loirin stood there, holding a fussy baby in her arms. Loirin stilled as well, her eyes widening at the sight of them.

Diana's heart leapt into her throat. This was it. Loirin would call for the others, and they would kill her and Artair.

But Loirin didn't move. When she spoke, her voice was low, barely above a whisper.

"There's a horse in the stables and a bag of supplies ye can use behind the counter. I never saw ye."

And with that, she turned to leave, disappearing into a side room.

CHAPTER 6

$\mathcal{A}$rtair gripped the reins of the horse they'd taken from the back stables of the inn, kicking the sides of the horse's flank to urge him to gallop faster. Diana had her arms wrapped around his waist from behind; he could feel her quick breaths against the back of his neck. He'd never ridden a horse so quickly in all his life, but he was eager to put as much distance between him, Diana, and those bastards as possible.

They'd been riding for just a short time, but the village was already far behind them. He didn't have a destination in mind as he still didn't know exactly where they were. Their surroundings only consisted of stretches of vast glens and patches of forest.

He drew in a sharp breath, wincing as a sharp pain from his bruised jaw pierced him. Tamhas, Iomhar, and the other men had demanded repeatedly that he tell them who he truly was, and why he'd come to the Scottish border. He'd maintained his story through every blow they'd rained down upon him, knowing that he could never tell them the truth. He'd been unable to fight back given his binds, but if he ever crossed their paths again . . . a dark pleasure filled him at the thought.

Diana tightened her grip on him, and a surge of protective anger raced through him, erasing all thoughts of dark pleasure. He didn't want to think about what Diana had done to get free, but if Iomhar had touched her . . .

He swallowed, clenching his jaw to stymie his fury. Now was not the time to dwell on thoughts of anger and revenge. He needed to find them shelter for the night and a place for Diana to get herself out of his time.

They soon approached a lone farmhouse with attached stables. The house appeared empty. No smoke billowed from its roof, and the windows were dark. Still, he had Diana linger behind with the horse as he ventured forward to check. It was indeed empty. They could stay for the night in the empty stables and leave at first light, hopefully before the owners returned.

He tied up the horse just outside the stables before he and Diana entered. It was still chilly inside, but it would have to do for the night.

"All right," he said, turning to face her. "Ye need tae get yerself out of here."

Diana blinked at him in surprise. "What?"

"Ye need tae use yer witchcraft tae get yerself

out of here and back tae yer own time," he repeated. A surprisingly sharp jab of pain struck him at the realization that he would never see her again, but he ignored it.

"I'm not going to leave you in the middle of nowhere. I haven't gotten you back to the right place, and we still don't know what year this is," Diana protested. "I promised Kensa that—"

"From their dress and manner of speech, I think we're in the correct time. We're near the border, Tamhas all but confirmed it when he was questioning me. I think he and his men may be one of many border gangs around this area—they're thieves and murderers," Artair interrupted. "Ye need tae get back tae yer own time—and tae safety. I still have the coin that yer aunt gave us. 'Tis a good thing she put hidden pockets into our clothing—those bastards would have taken it all. I can take care of myself as I make my way north."

"You can take care of yourself?" Diana demanded. "Which one of us untied the other and got us out of there?"

He scowled. "I would have been able tae handle it, lass."

She gave him a skeptical look, eyeing his bruised jaw. But her expression shifted, and she seemed to deflate, taking a step back from him.

"To be honest with you . . . I don't know if I can."

"What do ye mean?"

"I don't think I can travel through time using

just my magic . . . not without a portal. Kensa may be able to do that, but I'm still new to all of this."

"Ye can try," he said, reaching out to take her hands.

Her hands were cold, but they might as well have been hot irons for the sudden heat that seared him as he held them in his own. Her eyes remained locked with his, filled with uncertainty, until she gave him a jerky nod.

"If yer spell works, and ye get back tae yer own time—thank ye for taking on the risk of bringing me back," he said, forcing the words past his lips. *She needs tae leave,* he reminded himself. *'Tis not safe for her here.*

"I'd accept your gratitude if I got you back to the right place," she said, though she gave him a wavering smile.

Diana turned and stepped away from him, moving to the center of the stables. She closed her eyes, and he watched as she murmured the words of a spell.

"*Snàthain ùine, cluinn m 'ghairm. Snàithnean tìde, cluinn m'anam. Thoir stiùireadh dhomh gu sàbhailte tro do shlighe gu mo thìde.*"

He waited, tense, a strange sense of loss seizing him as he waited for her to vanish . . . but nothing happened.

She tried again, speaking the words of a different spell, but still, nothing happened.

Diana opened her eyes, frustration flitting across her face.

"I knew it wouldn't work," she muttered. "I even tried a Transport spell to apparate to another location—nothing. I'll keep practicing, but it looks like I'll have to use the portal in Tairseach to get back."

Artair knew he should feel disappointment that she hadn't been able to travel on her own, but it was relief that washed over him. Now they had to remain together until they reached the Highlands . . . and he'd have more time with the beautiful witch.

He met her eyes, trying to school his features into a look of disappointment.

"Very well, lass," he said gruffly. "We'll just have tae remain together till we reach the Highlands."

THEY MADE two large beds of straw to lie down on for the night, but it seemed as if the stables had grown even colder by the time they were done; he could see Diana shivering. She pulled her cloak more tightly around her; their sack of supplies included a thin blanket, but he knew it wouldn't be enough.

He straightened, eyeing her warily.

"Please donnae misunderstand what I'm about tae say, lass," he said. "But I think 'tis best we lie close together; our body heat will keep us warm."

Diana's face flamed as she met his eyes, but he saw no offense there, only reluctant agreement.

They found a comfortable position, their bodies pressed closely together, their arms wrapped around each other for extra heat. The feel of her lush body close to his caused an immediate reaction; he had to shift to make certain she didn't feel the evidence of his arousal. Even though they'd been riding all day, she smelled of sweet honey, the scent teasing his nostrils. They lay facing each other, her face barely grazing his shoulder, and he had to look down at her.

Her eyes were closed. As he studied her, he noticed a single tear fall from beneath her closed lids.

"Diana," he murmured, reaching out to tilt her face up to his. Her eyes flew open; they were indeed filled with tears. "What is it?"

"I got us into this," she whispered. "I took us to the wrong place—and they hurt you. If they come after us—"

"Nothing that has happened is yer fault," he said firmly. "Ye got us out of there when I couldnae —as ye just reminded me. All we need tae do is get ye back tae Tairseach. It will be a long trip north, but I ken Scotland; I've traveled a great deal down tae the Lowlands and back." He cocked his head to the side, studying her. "How did ye escape Iomhar?"

"Oh," Diana said, her face flaming as she lowered her gaze. "I—I seduced him. Well, I pretended to seduce him and implied I would lie with him if he let us go."

He wasn't prepared for the ferocious wave of jealousy that swept over him. He had to take a breath to quell his raging heartbeat.

"Did ye—"

"No. I didn't let him touch me," Diana interrupted. "I cast a Sleeping spell on him before he could kiss me."

This did little to quell his jealousy—jealousy that he reminded himself he had no right to feel.

"Artair?" Diana asked tentatively, taking in his stormy expression. "Are you all right?"

"Aye," he said, closing his eyes briefly to push aside the image of Iomhar touching Diana. "I just— I didnae want ye tae come tae any harm."

"I didn't," she insisted. "But thank God for that Sleeping spell."

Traces of anger still lingered within him; he needed to change the topic of conversation.

"Tell me something about yer life. Yer aunt mentioned ye were restoring an old home in the Highlands?"

"Yes. It's a manor that's belonged to my family for some time, but it's fallen into disuse. I like to visit it when my job and life in London get to be too much, and I need a bit of peace. It's a long way from being finished; I'll need to hire contractors to do the heavy lifting."

"What do ye handle in yer profession?" he asked. Kensa had told him that in the future, women had far more opportunities, and most of them had professions.

"I'm a solicitor," she said. "I handle property law."

He studied her face, but he saw no excitement, no passion for this profession.

"It pays the bills," she said with a shrug. "I think I'm mostly looking forward to the day I can retire and live in the manor I'm fixing up."

"Aye?" he asked. "Alone?"

"I'll have family visit—my Aunt Maggie. Kensa. And friends," she said with a trace of defensiveness in her tone. "But . . . I enjoy my solitude."

He couldn't deny the relief that filled him at her not mentioning a husband to join her in this manor, though he knew, like his earlier jealousy, he had no right to feel that way. And though her need for solitude was familiar—he often craved the same —it made him wonder why such a lovely lass wouldn't want to share her life with anyone.

"What about you?" she asked. "Are you looking forward to getting back to your life?"

"Aye," he said, though he felt no joy at the prospect. "Caitria is happy with the man she's found—I suspect she's far happier than she'd ever have been with me. Our marriage would have been a mistake. I'll eventually find someone tae wed, tae have my sons, but for now I'm content with my solitude—like ye, lass."

And he had been content with his life of solitude, his focus on duty. But that was before he met the golden-haired witch who smelled of honey, and whose touch seared him with heat. A witch who would soon vanish from his life and this time to the future in which she belonged.

"That woman who helped us—Loirin," Diana was saying, her brow furrowed. "I wonder why she helped us? Do you think her brothers are hurting her?"

"If they are, 'tis not our concern," he said firmly.

"I still wish we'd asked her to leave with us," Diana said. "She looked so frightened."

He surveyed her, reaching out to smooth the worried crease of her brow with his fingertip.

"I'm sure she can handle herself," he said. "She has a bairn. Perhaps that's why she remains with them. Ye're very kind, Diana. Tae think of someone else at a time like this."

She just gave him a shrug and a shy smile. Their eyes locked—and there it was again, the heat that roared to life inside him as if someone had lit a fire in his belly—a heat that threatened to swallow him whole.

He opened his mouth to urge her to get some rest, but there was a *wanting* in her eyes, and it seemed as if the chill around them had evaporated. Now he was only aware of the softness of her body against his, her parted lips, her flushed face. Her eyes lowered—just slightly—to his lips, and he couldn't hold back a moment longer. He needed a taste of her.

He leaned forward, capturing her lips with his. She melted into him, her mouth opening to his like the petals of a flower opening to the sun. He groaned as he explored her sweet mouth with his tongue. She let out a soft sigh, which only further ignited his arousal. He held her even closer, relishing in the feel of her hardened nipples against his chest through the layer of their clothes, eager to taste every part of her. He kissed her until they were both breathless, and when he finally—reluctantly—pulled back, her breathing was ragged, her eyes still alight with desire.

He wanted more, so much more, but he forced himself to rein in his desire. They were only together for the time being, for the purpose of going their separate ways.

"We need tae sleep," he forced himself to say. "We have a long journey ahead."

She blinked, as if coming out of a stupor, and nodded her agreement.

He held her in his arms as she drifted off, but he remained awake long after she fell asleep, his body awash with unrequited desire—and need.

CHAPTER 7

*D*iana awoke as shafts of sunlight filtered into the stables. Artair still slept next to her. She gazed at him, a smile touching her lips as a yearning filled her. He was a beautiful man—the sunlight illuminated his strong jaw and his long lashes, which looked golden in the light. She recalled his lips on hers the night before, and desire stirred within her. Unable to stop herself, she reached out to brush a stray strand of chestnut hair back from his face.

Artair stirred, his blue eyes flying open. His eyes met hers, and she swallowed, longing for him to pull her in his arms, to kiss her again . . .

"We should leave," he muttered, getting to his feet and breaking the spell.

"Right," she said, swallowing against the hurt that washed over her at his abruptness.

She stood to brush the straw from her gown as Artair reached into their sack of supplies and handed her a piece of bread. "We need tae keep moving north tae find another inn—and we need tae find out exactly where we are."

His tone was all business, to the point of being brusque, as if they were polite strangers as opposed to two people who'd traveled through time together, faced an immediate hostage situation, and then shared a steamy kiss.

But Diana nodded; he was absolutely right. The sooner they reached the Highlands, the sooner she could get to the portal, and he could get back to his life.

The bread was tasteless, but she forced herself to eat it all. Artair seemed to sense her distaste for the bread, telling her with a smile that they'd find a better meal at an inn.

When they mounted their horse, Artair rode at a more leisurely pace, though by the firm set of his muscles, she could tell he was still on guard. Diana prayed that Tamhas and his brother wouldn't attempt to pursue them further.

They rode until midday, and Diana found herself relaxing the farther north they rode. She wanted as much distance between them and Tamhas as possible. They didn't speak much, and the memory of their kiss raced through Diana's mind on an endless loop; she had to force herself to push the images aside.

They soon arrived at a bustling village that was larger than the one Tamhas and his men had taken them to. Artair asked a passing man for directions to the nearest inn, and they made their way to the center of the village where Artair handed the horse over to a stable boy, informing him that the horse needed to be watered and fed immediately, they had been riding for some time.

They paid for two rooms, and the innkeeper told them they were in the village of Lockerbie, not far from Dumfries. She noticed that Artair paled at the mention of Dumfries.

"What's in Dumfries?" she asked, as soon as they were alone in her room. "I saw your reaction when the innkeeper mentioned it."

"My sister and her husband," he said gruffly. "They're not in Dumfries, but just outside it. They have a home there."

"Perfect," Diana said, relief swelling inside her. "We can get more supplies and food for the journey north."

"I told ye before—my sister and I didnae part well. 'Tis been many years since we've spoken."

Diana studied the hesitation on his face.

"Do you want to see her?"

"Aye," he replied, after a long pause, though his expression remained tumultuous. "We'll go see her —but we'll stay here for the night."

He turned, moving to the door, still not looking at her.

"Get yerself a meal downstairs—whatever ye want. Yer aunt gave us plenty of coin. I'm going tae the local church."

Diana frowned. Though she knew people

from the medieval era were far more religious than in her time, it struck her as odd that Artair would feel the need to seek out a church, especially given that her status as a witch didn't seem to bother him. He seemed to find her magic intriguing, not evil.

He smiled at her startled expression, the tumult in his eyes vanishing.

"I want tae confirm the year. Record books at churches often have them listed. I donnae want tae alarm the innkeeper by asking him the year."

After he left, Diana moved over to the window, looking out at the bustling street as Artair disappeared among the crowds. Even if she hadn't gotten them exactly to the year 1390, given her scant knowledge of the time period, by the look of people's clothing and the village itself, it looked like she'd gotten them pretty close.

Despite her earlier self-admonishment for getting them to the wrong location, she'd still guided them back through time in one piece. A sudden swell of pride rose in her chest, along with a trace of wistful sadness. Her parents would have been proud of her.

She made her way downstairs, where she had a vegetable stew served with bread. She chose to eat in her room as the innkeeper and other guests openly stared at her when she spoke, and she didn't want to draw too much unnecessary attention.

Artair still hadn't returned when she'd finished eating. To quell her worry, she mentally reviewed some spells Kensa had taught her, spells that could come in handy during their travel north.

Artair returned to her room just as she was practicing how to light a candle with just her magic. She turned to face him, relieved at the sight of him.

"I'm sorry it took so long, lass," he said with an apologetic look. "I had tae ask for—"

"It's all right," she interrupted. "Well? What year are we in?"

He gave her a grave look, taking both her hands and leading her to the bed, sitting down opposite her. She swallowed, dread rising in her chest.

"Oh God. Please tell me we're not hundreds of years away from where we should be," she whispered. "It looks like we're in the fourteenth or fifteenth century, but I'm no historian, and—"

She stopped, realizing that Artair's mouth was twitching. He was trying not to laugh. She yanked her hands from his with a scowl.

"Artair. What year is it?"

"'Tis the year of our Lord, 1390," he said with a chuckle. "I was going tae jest with ye and tell ye we were in the ninth century, but I couldnae—yer face was filled with such fright."

Overwhelming relief washed over her, and she let out a laugh.

"That would have been cruel."

"Aye. 'Tis why I couldnae go through with the jest," he said, his expression turning serious. "Ye need tae have more belief in yerself, lass. It was ye

—not yer aunt—but ye who guided us safely back through time."

His tone was reverent, and Diana swallowed hard as the now familiar ache of desire wound its way through her body. She recalled his mouth on hers the night before, his strong body pressed against hers, and she ached for him to kiss her again.

But Artair was already on his feet, moving toward the door.

"Now that we ken what year we're in and where we are, the rest of our journey north should be much easier," he said. "Come down when ye're ready. I'll request another meal for us downstairs."

He was gone before she could reply.

DIANA STOOD IN A FOREST CLEARING, her heart pounding as she looked around. She didn't know where she was—but she sensed danger.

As she stumbled forward, she abruptly halted in her tracks. Two people hurried toward her—two very familiar people. She froze as they drew closer to her.

The two people were her parents. They were still a distance away, but she could make out her mother's familiar blond hair and brown eyes, her father's dark hair and blue eyes. Joy seized her, and she rushed toward them—but they halted, turning away from her.

And now Diana could see who they'd been running from. A group of men with painted faces who charged toward them. Panic coursed through Diana's veins; she opened her mouth to urge them to run.

But it was too late. The men shot multiple arrows at her parents, and they collapsed to the ground, their lifeless eyes staring up at the sky. Diana sank to her knees, screams of grief erupting from her.

"Diana!"

Diana awoke to Artair gently shaking her. She met his eyes, her breathing still ragged, her heart still racing, and it took several long moments to realize what she'd seen had just been a nightmare.

"'Tis all right, lass," he murmured, pulling her into his arms and rocking her as her pulse returned to normal. "Ye were just dreaming."

She closed her eyes, burrowing herself against his broad chest.

She dimly recalled the details of the evening before she'd retired to bed. They'd shared a polite dinner during which they'd only spoken of the journey to come, how much supplies they'd need, and how many stops they'd make, before retiring to their rooms with polite good nights. Yet the sexual tension between them still raged, and Diana had fallen asleep with an ache between her thighs.

"Do ye want tae tell me what it was about?" he asked, pulling back to gaze down into her eyes.

"It—was just a nightmare," she whispered,

closing her eyes against the horrible image of her parents' dead bodies riddled with spears. She didn't want to relive it; she just wanted to forget.

"All right," he said, reaching out to squeeze her hand. "Try tae rest."

He stood, and she spoke without thinking. "Can you—stay with me?"

Her voice was small, like a child's, and embarrassment flooded her.

"I mean, if it's not too much trouble to—"

"'Tis not," he said, with a gentle smile.

He settled down onto the bed next to her and pulled her close. The hum of desire roiled through her, but something else did as well. Comfort. A sense of safety—belonging. She'd never felt such a strong sense of safety before. It was what she needed after the horrible nightmare.

She didn't think she would be able to sleep, but soon found herself drifting off. This time, the images that filled her dreams were only of Artair, his naked body next to hers, his mouth on her lips, and that glorious sensation of *belonging*. That sense of home.

CHAPTER 8

*A*rtair shifted in the chair by Diana's bed, watching as she began to stir. He'd been unable to sleep beside her the night before, recalling the delicious feel of her mouth opening beneath his, and a firestorm of arousal had coursed through him. He'd wondered how it would feel to awaken her and claim her mouth, to taste her skin, to sink inside of her, and the thoughts had aroused him to the point of discomfort.

Guilt had slithered through him—the lass had suffered through a terrible nightmare, and he couldn't think past his desire. He had to force himself out of bed and into the chair, hoping it would quell his need for her. It hadn't, but he'd remained stubbornly in the chair, drifting off to sleep whenever he could.

He watched as Diana awoke and turned to face him, the sleeve of her underdress slipping to reveal the curve of her bare shoulder.

"Good morning tae ye, lass," he said gruffly. "Did ye sleep well?"

Diana nodded and sat up, causing the sleeve of her underdress to slip a little more, revealing even more of her shoulder, and he had to grit his teeth against the ache that flared to life inside of him at the sight.

"Thank you for staying with me."

"Aye," he said, getting to his feet and stretching; his muscles ached from spending the night in the chair.

Diana studied him, her eyes widening. "Did you sleep all night on that chair?"

"No," he lied. She didn't need to know that his desire for her had forced him out of bed. "I awoke shortly before you."

She smiled, her lips curving, and he allowed himself to fantasize about seizing that lovely mouth with his own. But he forced himself to shove the tantalizing image away, moving to the door.

"We should be on our way."

As THEY RODE out of the village and west toward Dumfries, anxiety filled him at the thought of seeing his sister again, and his hands shook on his reins. He'd traveled through time—twice—yet he was more nervous about seeing his sister again.

He thought of the harsh words they'd exchanged the last time they'd seen each other, and regret filled him. Liosa had expressed frustration over Artair's increasing self-imposed isolation after their father's death; how he focused more on his duties as laird than on family or relationships. Her anger reached its apex when he began to turn down invitations to local clan gatherings and suppers.

"Soon ye'll have no one in yer life tae care for! Or who'll care about ye! Ye're becoming just like our father! He had no one at the end—no one but us!" Liosa had shouted.

"Are ye trying tae tell me something, sister?" Artair challenged. "I donnae consider it an insult tae be compared tae the father who loved us—"

"It wasnae meant tae be an insult—"

"Our father left the manor and our lands tae me; 'tis all my responsibility! I donnae need ye or anyone!" he roared.

Hurt entered his sister's eyes, and he regretted his words. But his pride ruled him in those days. He just continued to glare as Liosa's face flushed with pain and anger.

"All right, brother," she returned softly. "I'll give ye what ye desire—yer solitude."

She left the manor the next day. He thought she would calm down and return, but after one month passed, and then another, he realized his sister wasn't coming back. His pride and stubbornness prevented him from apologizing, from asking her to return.

She sent him letters over the years, letting him know of her whereabouts and giving him brief updates about her life, but those letters soon grew few and far between until they stopped altogether.

He had told himself that it was for the best, that his sister would be happier without him, but he'd felt the gaping chasm of her loss ever since.

He took a calming breath, telling himself that he'd just request supplies and continue on his way with Diana to the next inn. If Liosa sent him away, it was her right. He expected it.

They approached his sister's large manor on the outskirts of Dumfries, which he remembered the directions to from the last letter Liosa had ever sent him. He took in the expansive manor with a sense of relief; at least his sister had married well and was living in comfort.

He dismounted as they arrived on the narrow dirt path that led to the front door. Before they reached it, the door swung open and a red-haired man he didn't recognize stepped out and eyed him. From his fine clothing, Artair guessed he was the laird of the manor, his sister's husband and his brother-in-law, Laird Keagan Padarsan. A woman soon appeared at the man's side, and Artair stopped in his tracks as he gazed into the eyes of his sister Liosa for the first time in years.

She looked just as he remembered. They both possessed the same chestnut hair, only she had their late mother's dark eyes, not their father's blue. Beneath his nervousness, a sense of pride bloomed. His wee Liosa was a grown woman now, a lady of her own manor.

Liosa's face had gone white at the sight of him, and he thought he saw her sway a little on her feet. He stepped forward, forcing a wide smile.

"Liosa."

Liosa stepped out the front door, her focus only on Artair and not sparing Diana a glance. She reached him, her shocked expression giving way to a fiery anger. She lifted her hand—and slapped Artair hard.

Artair clutched his face, reeling. Liosa clutched her hand, her breath heaving, angry tears filling her eyes.

"Seven years and no word! Seven years and ye show up here out of nowhere!"

Liosa's voice broke and she began to weep, her shoulders shaking, and Artair's heart cracked with guilt and regret. He wanted to pull her into his arms, to apologize a thousand times, but he suspected that would earn him another slap. A well-deserved one.

Keagan hurried forward, pulling Liosa into his arms as she wept.

"I'm Keagan, yer sister's husband," he said, his expression cold and unfriendly. "I've heard a great deal about ye."

He suspected his sister had not told Keagan good things about him. He took a step back, swallowing hard. It was a mistake coming here.

"I—I'm sorry tae have caused ye such grief, Liosa," he muttered. "I'll take my leave."

He gestured for Diana to come with him. But

Diana subtly shook her head, giving him a look of disapproval. She moved close to him, lowering her voice.

"Artair, you shouldn't just leave her like this."

"She's right tae be angry. It was foolish of me tae come here."

He turned to make his way to their horse, but a voice stopped him.

"Artair Dalaigh," Liosa's voice still quavered with anger, but it was firmer now. "Ye donnae get tae walk away from me—not again. Ye're going tae stay—and ye've got some explaining tae do."

Liosa stared into the flames of the fireplace, her shoulders tense. Keagan had left them alone, and a maid had escorted Diana to a chamber to wash and change her clothes.

He'd told Liosa the same tale he'd told Tamhas and his men, that he'd been traveling north from England when the shared coach he'd taken with Diana was robbed by bandits. Together they were making their way to the Highlands: Diana to visit family, Artair back to his manor. He opted not to share the frightening hostage situation they'd found themselves in with the border men; he didn't want to needlessly worry his sister. Not after they hadn't seen each other for so long.

As he'd spoken, Liosa's expression didn't change, and she kept her gaze trained on the flames.

"Ye ken . . . I would be less angry if ye just told me the truth," she said finally.

He frowned. "The truth? I did. I told ye—"

"About ye and the Sassenach."

"Diana?"

"Aye," she said, with a trace of impatience. "Ye two are more than just wayward travelers. Is she yer mistress? Are ye bedding her?"

He was shocked to hear his wee sister speaking so plainly. *She's not wee anymore,* he reminded himself. She was a married woman. He lowered his eyes, surprised—and irritated—that his desire for Diana was so plain.

"I am telling ye the truth," he lied. "Diana's a lovely lass, aye, but I barely ken her. I'm escorting her tae the Highlands as 'tis not safe for a lass tae travel on her own."

Liosa still looked suspicious. His sister had always been perceptive, even when she was a bairn. He recalled a time when he'd tried to slip from the castle to join his friends to go riding instead of doing his lessons with the castle tutor. Liosa had caught him and questioned him until he'd had no choice but to confess—a confession which she'd promptly told their parents and the annoyed tutor. At the time, he'd been furious with his sister, but now an amused smile touched his lips at the memory. Liosa misconstrued the smile and glowered.

"I'm glad ye find this so amusing," she bit out.

"I wasnae laughing at ye," he said, his smile

vanishing. "Liosa, I ken I deserve yer anger. It was wrong of me tae not contact ye for so long. We just need supplies and we'll be on our way."

"Ah," Liosa said, hurt flashing across her face. "Ye just need something from me, and ye—"

"I was ashamed, Liosa," Artair interrupted.

Liosa stilled, falling silent.

"I—I was ashamed that I let my pride and stubbornness send ye away," he continued, his chest tightening. "I feared I'd driven ye away forever. I—I was going tae be content with marrying a clan chieftain's daughter, Caitria MacGreghor. The MacGreghors were going tae be my family. I thought it would at least help with my solitude; I donnae need love the way ye do. I thought yer life would be better without having tae concern yerself with yer stubborn brother."

"Then ye're a coward. Ye never turn yer back on family—never," she said firmly.

She expelled a breath, looking back down at the flames.

"Ye and yer Sassenach can stay the night for supper and supplies. Then ye should go on yer way."

CHAPTER 9

"We're about the same size as the lady of the manor. I'll fetch a gown of hers for ye tae wear," said Bernasa, a young maid, as she ushered Diana inside a large guest chamber.

Diana dutifully followed her into the chamber. She and Keagan had left Artair and his sister alone, and Keagan had directed Bernasa to find her a guest chamber and some clothes, for which she was grateful—the gown she'd traveled in from the twenty-first century was now dirty and torn from all the nonstop travel.

"Thank you," Diana said, taking in the chamber with quiet awe.

It was elegant and too large for just one person in her opinion, with wood-paneled floors, massive windows that looked out to the front grounds, and a bed opposite a brick fireplace that roared with a fire.

Bernasa left her with a polite bow and Diana sank down onto the bed with a shuddering breath, her thoughts turning to Artair. Though she knew Artair and his sister were estranged, she'd not expected that scene between the two of them. Even through Liosa's fury, Diana could tell that she loved her brother fiercely. In the dark days after her parents' deaths, Diana had longed for a sibling, someone who'd understand and share in her grief. She knew Artair and his sister had lost their father —shouldn't that have brought them closer? What had happened to separate the two of them?

It's none of your business, she scolded herself, as Bernasa reentered the chamber with a fine green gown and a wash basin.

"Let me help ye, my lady," Bernasa began, stepping forward, but Diana shook her head.

"I'm fine, thank you," she said hastily. "You can leave me."

A flicker of hurt surprise entered Bernasa's eyes, but she obliged with another polite bow. *People have servants who help them bathe and dress in this time,* Diana reminded herself. She would have to keep that in mind the longer she stayed in this time.

Once she was alone, she thoroughly washed her skin, shivering at the feel of the cool water. When she was clean, she changed into her new gown, which fit perfectly. Artair entered just moments after Bernasa took away her wash basin.

He'd washed up as well and now wore a white tunic and long belted kilt; it was the first time she'd seen him in one, and it fit him like a glove. He looked breathtakingly handsome. Her heart picked up its pace, and she had to fight to keep her expression neutral, not wanting him to see the effect he had on her.

"I take it you've spoken with your sister?" she asked.

"Aye," he said, his eyes a storm of conflict. "I'm sorry ye had tae witness that. I thought she would turn us away, but she's agreed to give us shelter for the night and provisions so we can continue on our way. 'Tis my pride that's kept us apart for so long; we'll never have the relationship we once did."

"How do you know?" Diana challenged, approaching him. "She's your sister—your only living family. She loves you—and you love her."

"Too much time has passed," he said, shaking his head.

"If I had a sibling—the only family I had left in the world—I would do everything I could to make things right," Diana said, holding his gaze.

"I thought ye craved yer solitude," Artair returned, quirking an eyebrow.

"That's because I've only known solitude," she said without thinking, and realized this was true.

Her Aunt Maggie had raised her after her parents' deaths, and she had Kensa. She loved them both, but neither relationship came close to the one she'd had with her parents. The few romantic relationships she'd had over the years had come and gone, and she had no close friends. She'd come to accept that she could—and would—rely only on herself.

Artair's expression changed to one of sympathy, before something unreadable flickered in his eyes.

"I donnae think ye'll always be alone, lass," he said. He reached out to touch the side of her face, and a spiral of warmth twisted inside her belly. "Ye're tae lovely of a lass tae be alone for long."

Diana's breath caught in her throat; she realized how close they stood together. The memory of his lips on hers in the stables seared itself onto her mind. His blue eyes bore into hers, and as he leaned forward, an *ache* filled her—an ache that could only be satisfied by Artair.

"The laird and lady want ye tae ken that supper will be served shortly," Bernasa's voice interrupted them from outside the door, shattering the heated moment.

Artair stepped back from her, blinking and clearing his throat.

"I'll see ye downstairs."

Diana closed her eyes as her racing heart eased its thunderous pace, wishing she knew a magical spell that could extinguish desire for a man she could never truly have.

∾

DIANA HAD NEVER BEEN to a tenser meal in her life. She and Artair sat across a silent Keagan and Liosa, while Bernasa scurried back and forth to refill their cups.

Artair was focused on his plate, just as silent as Keagan and Liosa, while Diana tried to enjoy her meal. While the food at the inn had been sufficient, this meal was downright succulent—spiced venison and roasted carrots with ale. But it was hard to enjoy her meal when she felt as if she were amid a silent war between Artair and Liosa.

"This is a lovely meal," Diana said finally, desperate to break the tension. "Thank you."

"Ye're most welcome," Liosa replied, though her tone was unfriendly. She leaned back in her chair, giving her an appraising look. "What part of England are ye from?"

"The south," Diana replied, trying to keep her tone light, despite the hammering of her heart.

"Yer accent is odd," Liosa said, narrowing her eyes. "Being so close tae the border, we've seen a good deal of English folk pass through. What is the name of yer village of birth?"

"Enough, Liosa. Donnae take yer anger at me out on Diana," Artair snapped.

"I just find it odd that a Sassenach travels with ye. One who is no doubt pleased tae have caught herself a Highland laird."

Diana looked at Liosa in disbelief. Of all the accusations she'd expected to come her way, this wasn't one of them.

"Liosa," Artair hissed, glaring at his sister.

"I may be furious with my brother, and we may not have spoken in a long while, but he's the only family I have, and I'll still look out for him. I can tell ye're lying about something and I donnae trust ye. I'll not let him get taken in by a Sassenach whore who—"

"Enough!" Artair bellowed, getting to his feet. He reached down and helped a shaking Diana to her feet. "We may be guests in yer home, but I'll not sit here and let ye insult Diana. We're happy tae return when ye apologize."

Liosa had the good sense to look regretful, but Diana still shot her a glare as she and Artair left the room. He led her upstairs to her guest chamber, giving her a look of apology.

"I'm sorry, Diana," he muttered. "I didnae expect her tae take her anger out on ye."

"You don't have to apologize," Diana said, lowering her voice. "But Artair, may I suggest telling her the truth? Or at least part of it? You trust your sister, don't you?"

While Liosa's words still annoyed Diana, she knew her anger must have stemmed from her hurt over Artair's estrangement. And she obviously hadn't bought their story. Perhaps some part of the truth would assuage Liosa's hostility.

"With my life," he replied. "But 'tis not that simple, Diana. We donnae have the same relationship we once did. And I cannae tell her we've traveled through time—I have no doubt she'd send us away if—"

"Then tell her about those men at the border who took us hostage. We're here for one more night, Artair. Maybe you can use it to bridge the gap between the two of you."

CHAPTER 10

Though he tried to heed Diana's words as he walked back to the dining room, his anger at his sister hadn't dissipated. As soon as he entered the room, he glared at Liosa. He noticed that Keagan wasn't there; he wondered if his absence was purposeful.

"How dare ye—" he began.

But Liosa stood, holding up her hands in a gesture of supplication.

"Ye're right," she interrupted. "I regretted the words as soon as they slipped from my lips."

He fell silent, studying his sister with surprise. With her stubborn streak, he'd never known Liosa to apologize so readily. As if reading his thoughts, she gave him a small smile.

"I'm not the stubborn wee lass ye once kent, brother," she said.

He couldn't help but smile back, his anger

fading. Perhaps Diana was right, and she did deserve some part of the truth.

"I should apologize as well," he said. "Ye were right. I havenae been fully truthful with ye."

Liosa's eyes widened, filling not with anger—but triumph.

"I could tell as soon as I saw you two there was something more. What is it? Is she yer mistress? Is she with child? Are ye secretly wed because she's a Sassenach and the northern clans willnae accept her? Is that why ye were in England? Is—"

"Liosa," he interrupted, chuckling at Liosa's creative assumptions, though her words did put the tempting image of Diana, swollen with his child, in his mind. "None of those are true. What is true is that we were taken hostage by a group of border men. They were suspicious of a Highlander and a Sassenach traveling through their lands—but we managed tae get away from them."

Liosa paled at his words.

"Border men?" she asked. "What did they look like?"

"There were at least a dozen of them. But their leader's name is Tamhas. Do . . . ye ken them?" he asked, alarm prickling along his spine.

"No," Liosa said quickly, though the word seemed forced. "I thank ye for telling me the truth, brother. I'm glad ye managed tae get away from them." She cocked her head to the side, giving him a long look. "And there's nothing between ye and Diana?"

He swallowed hard; damn his sister's keen perception. But if he wanted her to forgive him, to open up to him, he needed to be more truthful with her.

"I've kissed her," he admitted, lowering his gaze. It was odd to discuss such matters with his sister. "But nothing more will happen. I'm accompanying her tae the Highlands, nothing more."

Liosa quirked an eyebrow.

"Ye were never a good liar," she said with a light laugh. "Especially when ye try tae lie tae yerself."

HIS SISTER WAS RIGHT—HE was lying to himself. He craved Diana more than he had any other lass. That night, images of Diana filled his dreams. Diana holding his hand as she led him into a dark, swirling abyss, urging him to trust her. His lips pressed to hers and then trailing down the smooth expanse of her skin. Her laughing brown eyes as she looked up at him.

He awoke with a swollen cock and had to grit his teeth against the swell of pure need that arose within him. Not only was Diana a witch, she was a damned temptress. He just needed to get her back to Tairseach, and with time, she would fade from his mind.

He got out of bed, halting in his tracks when he noticed that the world outside his windows was filled with nothing but pure white. Unease coiled around him as he moved closer to the windows.

A thick snow blanketed the grounds, and even more snow fell. He closed his eyes. There would be no traveling in this weather.

"Artair?"

He heard Diana's hesitant voice outside his door. Striding over to it, he found Diana standing there, clad only in her underdress and a wool cloak. She moved past him, crossing over to the window.

"We're not going anywhere soon, are we?" she asked, heaving a sigh. "It seems like I'm going to be trapped in this time forever."

Genuine dismay shaped her words; a sharp reminder to him that she didn't want to be here in this time. Even as he told himself this, his cock stirred at the sight of her: she wore her golden locks loose over her shoulders, and the outline of her breasts beneath her underdress was downright distracting. He forced himself to avert his gaze.

"Ye will. Ye have my word, lass. We'll get ye tae Tairseach."

She turned to him with a wry smile.

"I'm supposed to be the one getting you home, remember?"

"Ye got us to this time, Diana," he reminded her. "I can get us north. We should get dressed and see my sister," he added, trying not to stare at the tempting curve of her breasts. He needed to get her out of his chamber.

Diana looked a little hurt at his dismissal, but

she nodded her agreement and left. Once she'd left, he briefly closed his eyes and moved over to the window. It seemed as if fate were mocking him by forcing him to remain in such proximity with the tempting lass he desired.

He dressed and went downstairs to find Liosa setting the table. Bernasa was nowhere to be seen.

"It looks like ye and yer English lass are stuck here, brother," Liosa said wryly. "I sent the servants home last night to tend tae their own families during this storm; we're on our own till it clears."

Diana entered the room then, looking even more lovely in a light blue gown. She took in Liosa setting the table and stepped forward.

"Let me help you," she offered.

"There's no need, ye're my guest," Liosa said, her tone cool. "Please, sit down. Both of ye."

He scowled, not liking her cool attitude toward Diana, but opted to stay silent. They'd made good progress last night; he didn't want to fray their strained peace.

When Keagan joined them, they sat down to a meal of venison stew.

"If this storm lasts for days, we may use up our stores," Keagan said, giving Liosa a worried look.

"We can discuss such matters when our guests arenae present," Liosa returned, not looking up from her plate.

Artair stilled, surveying the sudden tension in his sister—her tight shoulders, her pale face. A household this size shouldn't run out of food stores so quickly.

"Are ye low on food?" he asked. When his sister didn't answer, he pressed. "Liosa?"

"'Tis not yer concern, Artair," she replied shortly.

He exchanged a look with Diana, who gave him a subtle shake of her head. But Artair's instincts were on fire—there was something going on here, something more than just low food stores. He could tell by Liosa and Keagan's mutual tension.

"If ye need help with something—if there are debts, or—" he continued.

"I said 'tis none of yer concern," Liosa snapped. "Ye cannae show up here after all these years and—"

"'Tis my concern," Artair snapped. "Ye're my sister."

"Am I?" Liosa returned with a bitter laugh. "I assumed ye'd forgotten."

He glared at her, and she returned it; the tentative peace between them now shattered.

"I'm no longer hungry, and I need tae tend tae the next meal," Liosa muttered, getting to her feet.

Keagan trailed her out of the room after shooting Artair a dark look. When he left, Artair turned to Diana, who also gave him a look of annoyance.

"And ye as well, lass? Are ye upset with me?"

"I may have been an only child, but I'm going to assume that taking a domineering attitude with your sister isn't going to make her open up to you.

I'm sure she'll tell you what's going on—but you've been apart for many years. You can't press her too much."

Artair glowered, wanting to tell Diana that he could handle his sister on his own, but he bit back a retort.

"Especially," she continued, "considering that we may have to be here for a few days. It's not like there are snow plow trucks in this time."

He didn't know what a truck was but didn't press.

He wanted to go after his sister and demand to know what she was hiding from him. Yet he had to grudgingly concede that Diana was right. Pushing Liosa on the matter would only make matters worse.

Diana got to her feet, moving over to one of the large windows in the dining room and peering out. She seemed lost in her thoughts, and curiosity propelled him out of his chair to approach her.

"What are ye thinking of?" he asked. "If 'tis about me and Liosa, ye're right. I'll—"

"No," she said. "I've already said my piece about that. I was just thinking about how beautiful this is. It snows in London, of course, but there's nothing like snow in the Scottish countryside. My parents would take me up to the Highlands for Yule when I was smaller, and they would lie down on the ground with me to make snow angels. It's one of my favorite memories."

She smiled, her eyes lighting up at the memory.

"Liosa and I would do the same, though our maid would scold us, telling us we'd catch a fever," he murmured, taking in the snow. "Sometimes we'd sneak out tae play in the snow with the servants' bairns."

"Snow is magical for children, isn't it?" Diana asked, raising her lovely eyes to his with a chuckle.

"Aye," he said. "Do ye want them? Bairns?"

He didn't know where the question came from, but he suddenly had a burning desire to know. Diana swallowed, returning her focus to the snow.

"No," she said, and his chest clenched at her words. "This—ability of mine—I don't want to pass the burden of magic onto a child. I know the dark side of what my power can do."

Pain tightened her expression; he wanted nothing more than to take it away.

"I donnae think yer witchcraft—yer magic—is a burden," he murmured. "I think 'tis a part of ye. I think it makes ye special. But there are other special things about ye as well. Ye have a good heart, tae have agreed tae transport me tae the past. And . . . ye're lovely, lass. The loveliest I've ever seen. It would be a shame not tae pass those traits on tae a bairn of yer own."

Diana turned to face him, a flush spreading across her cheeks. Again, the image of Diana swollen with child—his child—entered his mind, and the desire that followed the image made him reach up to gently grip her nape, to press her close to him, to delve into her sweet mouth with his tongue.

His desire for her consumed him; he didn't care that he was in his sister's dining room—he wanted to take her where she stood, to lower the bodice of her gown and taste her lovely breasts before letting his fingers drift down to stroke her center.

"I want ye, lass," he murmured, tearing his mouth from hers to pepper kisses along her jaw, down to her throat. She let out a soft whimper, and he pulled her closer. "I donnae care that ye donnae belong in this time. I ache for ye, Diana, my golden witch. I can hardly breathe around ye."

"Artair," she whispered, arching her throat as he suckled the skin at its base. "I want you too. So much. But—"

She took a breath, stepping back and robbing him of her delicious heat.

"But I was sent back with you to guide you back home," she said, not looking at him as she spoke. "And that is what—and all—that I'll do. We've been sidetracked enough. My—my magic is still new. I can't let myself get distracted by how much I want you."

"Diana—" he whispered, stepping forward, but she took another step back; the movement splintered his heart.

"I'm sorry," she whispered, and hurried out of the room, leaving him alone and aching in her wake.

CHAPTER 11

I *want ye, lass.*

Artair's words filled her with longing. She could still barely breathe when she returned to her own chamber. *It's just desire*, she told herself. Searing, off-the-charts desire, but desire nonetheless. It was bad enough that she wanted him, but actually making love to him—the thought of which sent a maelstrom of heat careening throughout her body—would make her start to feel things for a man born centuries before her.

It had taken everything in her power to walk away from Artair, to not give in to the passionate need that raced through her. She needed to focus, to get him back to his manor and then back to her own time.

She pushed aside the memory of Artair's lips on her throat, the feel of his broad, muscular body pressed flush against her own. She should try to use the extra time she had here in the manor to strengthen her magical skills and practice spells.

Diana locked the door to make certain no one would interrupt her. Artair's sister seemed to distrust her. She could only imagine Liosa's reaction if she found Diana attempting to perform spells. A rule she had heard time and time again from her parents was to never openly practice magic in the superstitious past.

But as she tried to recite basic spells from memory, she found that she couldn't concentrate. Her traitorous mind kept filling with thoughts of Artair, of the raw desire in his blue eyes as he kissed her. *I ache for ye, Diana, my golden witch.*

She closed her eyes, expelling a sigh. It would do no good attempting to practice when all she could think about was Artair. She could still make herself useful, and though she was unlikely to ever see Artair's sister again once she left here, she was determined to get Liosa to like her.

She went in search of Liosa, finding her in the large kitchens in the rear of the manor. Liosa was concentrating on chopping vegetables as Diana stepped inside.

"Is there anything I can do to help?" Diana asked.

Liosa didn't look up.

"No, ye're our guest. Please—return tae yer chamber."

Frustration roiled through Diana, but she looked around, spotting an apron hanging in the kitchen's corner—one that didn't look too different from a modern-day apron. She put it on and stepped forward.

"I insist," Diana said firmly.

Liosa stopped chopping, glancing up at her, and for a split-second Diana thought she saw a glimmer of admiration in the other woman's eyes.

"All right," Liosa muttered, returning her attention to the vegetables. "Ye can cut up those squash over there."

Feeling a ridiculous amount of triumph, Diana moved over to the far end of the counter where a pile of winter squash sat and dutifully began to chop. They worked in silence for several long moments before Liosa spoke.

"Ye care for my brother," she said, still not looking up. It was a statement, not a question.

Diana flushed, but knew it was best to be honest.

"Yes," she said.

She waited for a follow-up question, her heart hammering in her chest, but to her relief there wasn't one. Liosa was now resolutely focused on dicing a pile of carrots.

"What was Artair like?" Diana asked, hungry for more knowledge about the man she desired so much. "When he was a child?"

"The opposite of the way he is now," Liosa said after a brief pause, a nostalgic smile tugging at her lips. "Loquacious. Always telling tales. My father used tae say he was a born storyteller."

Diana smiled, trying to imagine a cheerful young Artair telling Liosa stories.

"I was frightened of horses when I was younger, so he used tae tell me he could speak tae them. According tae Artair, they told him they would never hurt me. I kent he wasnae being truthful, but it eased my fears."

Diana chuckled in amusement.

"I never had siblings," she confessed. "It's stories like yours that make me wish I had."

"'Tis just ye and yer parents then?" Liosa asked, glancing up at her.

"Yes. My parents died some time ago," she said, a twinge of grief piercing her.

Diana felt Liosa's eyes on her as she focused on the squash. She stilled, looking up at the feel of a gentle pressure on her arm. Liosa stood there, her hand on her arm.

"I'm sorry," Liosa said with an empathetic smile. "My mother died when I was too young to remember, but I do remember how painful it was when my father died."

Diana returned her smile, and Liosa retreated back to her side of the kitchen. Something seemed to shift between them after that moment; she noticed that Liosa seemed less tense as she chopped.

They worked in companionable silence until Liosa insisted that she leave and wash up for the next meal, but this time she spoke with a genuine smile.

When Diana entered the dining room for evening supper, she felt considerably more relaxed, though she avoided the heat of Artair's gaze on her when he entered the room with Keagan. When she did look up, she noticed that both Artair and Keagan's expressions were tight with tension; she wondered what had happened between the two.

As they ate, Liosa filled up most of the silence with small talk, but Diana noticed Artair's increasing tension. His jaw was tight, and he barely ate. She swallowed hard, wondering if his tension was caused by her rejection after their kiss.

"Diana, will ye leave us for a moment?" he asked abruptly. "There's something I wish tae discuss with my family."

She was surprised at the hurt that pierced her at his words, words that reminded her of what an outsider she was. But stubbornness kept her rooted to the spot.

"I insist on staying," she said, bracing herself, certain that Liosa would demand that she leave. Yet Liosa remained silent, and when she glanced over at the other woman, she again caught a brief glimpse of admiration in her eyes.

Artair glared at her, his eyes flashing, but he also didn't protest. Instead, he turned his focus to Keagan and Liosa.

"Ye're both hiding something from me. I want tae ken what it is."

Diana frowned in surprise. Keagan and Liosa stiffened, avoiding his gaze.

"'Tis not yer concern—" Keagan began.

"Stop saying that," Artair interrupted. "Aye, I ken I havenae been in touch, but that doesnae mean I donnae care about my sister and what happens tae her. Now tell me what it is."

"Artair—" Diana interjected, but Liosa held up her hand.

"Very well," she murmured.

"'Tis our business, wife," Keagan hissed, but Liosa was focused on Artair.

"We've been having trouble with some border men. Usually they donnae venture this far north, but in the past few months they've been stealing our horses, cattle and food stores. One of them—he has a taste for the lassies—he's threatened tae harm me if we donnae give his men more of our stores."

A heavy silence fell. Keagan stared at the table, his jaw clenched. Liosa evenly held Artair's gaze, though she'd gone pale. Diana looked at Artair and flinched—she'd never seen him look so furious.

"What are these men's names?" Artair demanded.

"Artair, 'tis not—" Liosa began.

"What. Are. Their. Names?" he repeated.

"Tamhas and Iomhar. They're brothers," Liosa whispered.

Diana stilled, a chill spreading throughout her body. How was it possible that Liosa and Keagan were dealing with the exact same men she and Artair had encountered?

And then she recalled something Kensa had

once told her, how traveling through time made things . . . come together. How it increased the possibility of what seemed like coincidence. She'd told her that the men and women she sent back in time always ended up near their fated mates.

Perhaps they hadn't arrived at the border and near Liosa's home by coincidence. Perhaps it was purposeful—and they were meant to arrive here, to get caught by those men. Perhaps Artair's desire to reconnect with his sister was so powerful that the threads of time had sent them here instead of to his manor.

"Do ye have men who can help ye?" Artair asked, pulling her from the whirlwind of her thoughts.

"We're not like yer Highland clans," Keagan snapped. "I can protect my wife, my home."

"Ye clearly cannae," Artair returned, and Keagan shot to his feet.

"Ye cannae come into my home and presume—"

"Stop it, please," Liosa pleaded. "Yes, we have men from the other farms who help us. The border men have been nuisances for months, but we can handle them. Now—let's just finish our meal."

Artair's mouth tightened, and she could tell he wanted to protest, but Liosa's pale, pleading face was insistent. He grunted his agreement but was silent for the rest of the meal.

"I've prepared another course," Liosa said, with

forced cheerfulness. "Salted herring. One of yer favorites, Artair."

But Artair was already on his feet.

"My belly is full," he said shortly, before leaving the room.

Diana gave them an apologetic look and hurried after him as he entered the empty drawing room. He moved to the fireplace, looking down at the flames.

"How is it possible? That the same men who took us hostage—" he began.

"I was wondering the same thing," she interrupted. "I've been thinking—maybe time pulled us here because we're supposed to be here. Were you thinking of your sister before we traveled?" she asked.

"I was thinking of how good yer hands felt in mine," he said. There was no heat in his tone; it was a matter-of-fact statement. Still, her face warmed. "And then . . . aye. I was thinking of her. I wondered if she was worried about me; if she kent that I was missing, and I felt regret over our estrangement. Ye're saying that time—fate—wanted us tae be here?"

"I think so," Diana said.

"Then 'tis settled. I donnae care what my stubborn sister says—as soon as I get ye back to Tairseach, I'm returning with my best men tae fight those bastards."

As soon as I get ye back tae Tairseach. Diana forced a smile and gave him a nod. That was what she wanted—she didn't belong in this time. And Artair was perfectly capable of protecting his sister —his family—which she wasn't a part of.

"Are ye all right, lass?" he asked. "Donnae worry, I'll help get ye back—"

"Everything's fine," she said with another forced smile. "I'm glad you're going to help your sister. I want you to. I—I should get back."

She hurried out of the room before he could see the storm of conflicting emotions on her face, the same emotions that tore at her heart.

CHAPTER 12

*T*he snowstorm continued, with each day seeming to bring more snow. As the days passed, Artair decided not to tell his proud sister and brother-in-law that he had every intention of defending them from the border men, no matter what they said. Instead, as he spent his time helping out with tasks that needed tending to around the manor, he focused on getting to know his brother-in-law more and spending time with his sister—all the while trying to subdue his growing need for Diana.

"My wife is starting tae like yer mistress," Keagan said one morning, as Artair helped him gather chopped wood from the cellar to carry upstairs.

"Diana's not my mistress," Artair corrected.

Keagan gave him a look of skepticism, but said nothing, hefting a stack of wood into his arms and

107

heading toward the stairs. Artair followed, hoping he wouldn't continue to question him about Diana.

Keagan led him into the parlor where the fire burning in the fireplace had started to die out. They tossed several pieces of wood inside, and Keagan leaned over to restart the fire with flint and steel, using thistledown to help it roar back to life.

"I kent I wanted Liosa the moment I laid eyes on her," Keagan said after a long pause. "There was no need tae deny my desire for her."

Artair tensed; his implication was clear.

"I'll say it again—Diana isnae my mistress. And I ken my sister is a grown woman now, but I donnae wish tae hear how ye—"

"That's all I'll say," Keagan said, holding up his hands. "And I feel more than desire for yer sister. She's my life. I love her with every breath in my body."

"I ken ye do," Artair said, his expression softening.

He'd observed his sister and Keagan together. The smiles they shared, their gentle exchange of touches and kisses when they thought no one was looking. It caused an odd flare of envy to ignite in his belly, one which he had to temper every time he thought of Diana. Keagan and Liosa were in a different situation—they were wed, and they both were born in the same century.

"May I ask why ye have no bairns?" he asked now, pushing aside his thoughts of Diana.

Keagan stiffened, pain flaring in his eyes.

"I donnae mean tae pry—" Artair began.

"We've tried," Keagan said, his mouth twisting in a bitter smile. "God hasnae seen fit tae bless us with a bairn."

Keagan shifted his focus to picking up the unused wood and heading out of the parlor, but Artair could see the lingering pain in his eyes. He may not have known Keagan for long, but he could tell he was a good man. He'd learned that Keagan had grown up here, but moved to Dumfries to work as a merchant, as his older brother had inherited the manor. He'd only become laird of the manor after his brother's sudden death from illness, and like Artair, he'd suddenly had to take on the responsibility of managing a household and lands. But Keagan had told him that with Liosa's help, it had been an easy task.

At Keagan's request, he didn't bring up the couple's lack of bairns to Liosa—nor did he want to. Tension lingered between them, but Artair was determined to make peace with her. Liosa spent much of her time in the kitchens with Diana, preparing all the meals while the servants were away. So, he volunteered to bring up sacks of barley and other stores of food from the cellar and into the kitchens, taking pains to linger and converse with his sister while trying not to focus on how lovely Diana looked, how she seemed to fit right in with his sister, his family.

During one of his stops in the kitchen, Liosa told him how she'd met Keagan. She'd briefly lived with a distant relative of theirs in the southern Highlands. That was where she'd met Keagan, who was visiting his own relatives in the area.

"I kent as soon as I saw him that I would marry him," she said, a nostalgic smile lighting up her face. "He asked for my hand a fortnight after we met."

"And ye've been the lady of his manor since?" he asked.

"Aye. 'Tis wasnae much of a home when I first came here—it belonged tae an older brother of Keagan's who passed from illness some years ago. Together we made it into a home. It was what I tried tae tell ye years ago, brother," Liosa said, her eyes filling with emotion. "A home is more than just stones and bricks and servants. 'Tis where love is."

He stiffened, suddenly feeling exposed in front of Diana. He wanted to tell Liosa that if he chose to live his life in solitude, it was his choice to make, but the words wouldn't come—not with Diana standing there. And the walls his sister had put up were coming down; she hadn't spoken to him with such emotion in days. There was no use in starting an argument, so he gave his sister a nod.

"Ye're right," he said. "I—I should get back tae helping Keagan tend tae the fires."

Diana found him later in one of the upstairs chambers, stacking more wood into the fireplace.

"She's right, you know," she said with a small smile. "A home is more than just stones and bricks.

Is that the reason for your estrangement? She wanted you to find someone to love?"

He wanted to tell Diana that his relationship with his sister was none of her concern, but gritted his teeth instead. He straightened and faced her.

"She was concerned with my growing solitude, aye," he muttered. "I told her I didnae need her or anyone. I've regretted those words ever since."

"I'm sure she knows that." She hesitated, stepping forward. "I need to take a break from kitchen work. Since it's snowing like mad outside, would you like to take a walk with me around the manor?"

"Aye," he said without hesitation.

In his more prideful days, he would have refused, reminding her of her rejection when he'd confessed his desire for her. But he ached to spend time with Diana—his need to be around her went beyond his physical desire for her.

After that day's walk, they began to take daily walks around the manor, during which he shared stories of his childhood relationship with Liosa.

"What was your father like?" Diana asked, as they paused from their walk to gaze out the large windows at the end of the second-floor hallway.

"He was taciturn. Strict. He didnae spend much time with us, but I kent he loved us. As we loved him. I think my mother's death broke him. He chose to spend much of his time alone."

Diana arched an eyebrow. "That sounds familiar."

He tensed, considering. He'd never before

drawn the parallels between himself and his father, Laird Canron Dalaigh. Or perhaps he'd never allowed himself to, though Liosa had once accused him of becoming like his father.

Did he want to share his father's fate, dying alone, after a lifetime of emotional distance from his children?

"Tell me more about yer time," he said, not wanting to dwell on the disturbing thought. "What is London of the future like?"

"Large," she replied, after a long pause, and he was relieved that she didn't press him further about his father. "Larger than you could imagine—overflowing with people. It's why I often came to the Scottish Highlands to relax. I was looking forward to this particular holiday—until my aunt begged me to escort a certain Highlander back through time."

He grinned, his mood lightening.

"But he's a pleasure tae be around, isnae he? This Highlander?"

"I haven't decided yet," she replied, playfully narrowing her eyes, and he laughed.

He found out more about Diana during their walks—and meals together. She told him about the aspects of her job as a solicitor, her home in London which she called a "flat." He noticed there was no eagerness in her tone about her life in the future—there was a distance, as if she were speaking of someone else's life.

One evening after supper, and Liosa and Keagan had retired for the night, he decided to ask her about something she seemed to have passion for, even if she doubted her abilities. Her witchcraft.

"What is it like? Tae be able tae perform spells?"

His instincts were right; her face lit up at the question. She cocked her head to the side, nibbling on her bottom lip. For a brief, heated moment, he imagined suckling on that lovely lip, but forced himself to look at her eyes.

"I don't know how to describe it," she said.

He stood, crossing over to her and pulling her to her feet; it was just an excuse to touch her.

"Well," he said. "Why donnae ye show me?"

He was standing so close to her that her natural honeyed scent wafted into his nostrils. His breath hitched in his throat; he had to concentrate on her words.

"It feels like . . . electricity. Coiling around inside you."

He frowned. Kensa had tried to explain the concept of "electricity," but he still found it hard to understand.

"I donnae understand, lass."

Diana bit her lip, glancing down at the fire.

"Like . . . fire. A crackling beneath the skin. A sense of power flowing throughout your body," she said.

She reached out to touch his arm, running her hand along it, and every sense in his body roared to life.

"That must be quite the feeling," he murmured, trying to keep his voice steady.

"It is," she whispered.

Silence stretched between them, a silence fraught with desire. As their eyes locked, Artair succumbed to his need for her, reaching up to grab her by the nape and claiming her mouth with his own.

She wrapped her arms around him, returning his kiss with a wild ferocity, and he maneuvered her backward until he had her pressed flush against the wall. He pulled her body even closer to his so that she could feel the full force of his arousal.

Diana gasped into his mouth, and he reluctantly released her mouth, though he kept her within the circle of his arms.

"Lass, if ye donnae want this, I need ye tae tell me now," he rasped. "I ken ye told me that ye need tae focus on getting back tae yer own time, on yer magic, but—"

She interrupted him with a kiss, and when she pulled back, her own eyes were pools of desire.

"It was foolish of me to tell you that," she whispered. "Artair Dalaigh . . . don't you dare stop."

CHAPTER 13

*A*rtair let out a low, sexy growl at her words and crushed his mouth to hers. Diana reveled in the heat that swept over her body, the moisture that seeped between her thighs, her thundering heartbeat. She let out a yelp of surprise as he swung her up into his arms, carrying her out of the dining room.

"Liosa and Keagan—" she whispered.

"Already asleep in their chamber," he murmured. "And 'tis a good thing, witch. I intend tae make ye scream."

Delight rippled through her, and she wound her arms around his neck as he marched with her up the stairs as if she weighed nothing and into his chamber.

He once again seized her mouth as he strode with her to the bed. She moaned into his mouth, aching for him.

He released her mouth to lower her to the bed, and she let out a whimper of disappointment.

"Patience, my Diana," he murmured, stripping himself of his tunic and kilt. She took in his nude form and swallowed. He was as beautiful as she'd imagined—a broad muscular torso that led down to tapered thighs, and—

He grinned as her eyes widened when she took in the size of him.

"Not tae worry, witch," he murmured. "I'll be gentle with ye."

"No," Diana said, and he froze, looking down at her with surprise. She gave him a teasing smile. "Don't be gentle."

"Temptress," he growled, reaching out to strip her of her gown, his gaze tracking over every inch of her naked body. "Ye're beautiful, lass. My golden witch. My Diana."

Her heart leapt at his words. He leaned forward with a moan and seized one of her aching nipples into his mouth, laving it with his tongue as she gasped and arched beneath him, spirals of pleasure winding throughout her body. He turned his focus to her other breast, eliciting more fervent whimpers from Diana.

While he suckled upon her, his finger drifted down to dip into her center, and she let out a cry. He continued to stroke her center, and her pleasure gradually increased until it became difficult to breathe. She threw her head back, and just when she was on the verge of climax, he removed his finger.

"Artair—" She let out on a gasp of disappointment, but he lifted his mouth from her breasts to silence her protest with a kiss.

"Not yet, my Diana," he murmured. "I want ye tae come while I taste ye—I want tae taste yer sweetness in my mouth."

To demonstrate, he put his finger into his mouth, suckling, and the very sight caused a fiery need to corkscrew within her belly.

Keeping his blue eyes trained on hers, he peppered kisses down her abdomen until he reached the juncture of her thighs. He spread her legs wide, giving her a wicked grin as he clamped his mouth onto her center.

Diana let out a strangled moan as he feasted upon her. The sweet ache that had tormented her dissolved into pure pleasure, and she cried out as he moaned into her, gripping her buttocks to pull her even closer to his mouth. Diana had to place her hand over her mouth to stifle her screams, but Artair reached up to yank her hand away, his eyes hungry and demanding.

"I want tae hear every cry, every scream," he whispered, before returning to her mound to feast.

Diana obliged. Her whimpers and cries formed a litany as he continued to feast on her, and when her pleasure built to a climax she screamed, her body trembling wildly as he continued to lap away at her center.

"Artair," she whimpered. "Artair . . . "

He continued to lick her as her trembling subsided; only when she'd stilled did he rise up above her. She took in every inch of him—the tousled chestnut hair, the blue eyes filled with desire, his glorious nakedness—and she couldn't wait anymore, not one second more. She reached out to grip him by the buttocks, and he groaned as she guided him inside her.

The feel of him inside her almost made her come instantly; he stilled, as if sensing how close she was. And then, with a low growl, he began to move inside her, winding his hands through her hair and arching her head back to suckle at her neck as he thrusted.

"Artair," Diana whispered. "Oh God . . . "

"Ye're so tight, lass," he said with a groan, pulling her naked body even closer to his.

She relished in the feel of him against her as their bodies moved together in a steady rhythm, their heartbeats thundering in tandem. The pleasure that wound from her center to her entire body soon became too much to bear, and she let out a cry as another orgasm tore through her. Artair began to quake above her, and he shuddered, burying his lips into her hair, crying out his pleasure and release.

It took Diana several moments to catch her breath after Artair pulled out of her, still holding her within the circle of his arms. She was twenty-nine years old, and she'd never experienced love-making like that. The man knew how to work every inch of her body like a fine-tuned instrument, and in one session, he'd single-handedly ruined any sex she'd have in the future, though she pushed that troubling thought away.

When she opened her eyes, Artair was gazing down at her, his blue eyes twinkling.

"What thoughts are in that lovely head of yers?" he murmured.

"That you're terrible at lovemaking," she teased, and he laughed.

"Is that so, witch? Those two climaxes of yers would say otherwise."

She gave him a playful shove, her eyes roaming over his handsome face and his amazing body, which the firelight highlighted every inch of. Unable to stop herself, she reached out to touch the broad expanse of his chest and he let out a low rumble of pleasure. He reached out to take her hand, stopping its movement.

"Yer hand on my skin will bring my cock roaring tae life, witch," he murmured. "And I donnae think we can handle more lovemaking—not yet."

She just smiled, resting her head against his broad chest, struck by how *right* it felt to be in his arms. *I doubt this is what Kensa had in mind,* she thought with a grin.

"What amuses ye so?" he asked.

"My aunt probably didn't have this in mind," she said teasingly.

"No," he said with a wicked grin. "But I'm glad. I've wanted ye since I saw ye in those tight breeches ye wore when yer aunt first introduced us."

"You mean when you said I looked like a whore?" Diana asked, arching her brow, and Artair looked chastened.

"Ye'll have tae forgive me for that, lass. I was trying tae quell my desire for ye," he said, reaching out to run his hand through her hair. "I'm happy ye changed yer mind and agreed tae help me. I have tae ask—why is it ye're so reluctant tae use yer witchcraft? Most people would love tae have such a power."

Diana fell silent for a long moment. A part of her wanted to shut down, to not speak of the tragedy in her past, but a stronger part wanted to confide in him.

"My parents," she said finally. "I don't know how much Kensa told you, but after they died, I determined I would never travel through time. My parents died because of their magic. They traveled back to the past and ended up farther back in time than they intended—it's rare, but it can happen sometimes with Time-weaving spells. Members of a Pictish tribe happened to see them appear out of nowhere—and killed them on the spot."

Remnant grief flowed through her as she spoke, and Artair pulled her closer.

"The nightmare I had back at the inn—it was about their deaths. I've had many nightmares about it in the past, but I haven't had one in years. After they died, I begged another stiuireadh to travel back in time, to warn my parents not to go—or to save their lives. I even tried to do it myself, but Kensa warned me it was too dangerous, and it was a lost cause. My parents didn't belong in the time they ended up in, and because they didn't belong there, we could do nothing to prevent their deaths. I was furious with Kensa, with the other stiuireadh —and turned my back on time travel, magic—all of it. I figured—what was the point of having magic if I couldn't save the people I loved the most in the world?"

Tears pricked at her eyes, and Artair sat up, looking down at her.

"There is nothing ye could have done, lass," he murmured. "But I think they would be proud of ye now. Ye've grown into a woman with a kind heart— and magic ye use only tae help others." He lifted her hand to his lips, his eyes trained on hers. "I understand how the loss of a parent can hurt. But donnae let it define ye, Diana."

She rested her head on his shoulder and closed her eyes. Traveling to the past had begun to unravel her resistance toward magic and time travel. Hadn't it brought Artair into her life? She tried not to think of the fact that his presence in her life was tempo-rary, that she would return to her life and he to his.

121

Instead, she decided to focus on the time they did have together.

So, she curled into him, winding her arms around his neck.

"Make love to me again, Artair," she whispered, and he thoroughly obliged.

CHAPTER 14

*D*iana found it difficult to look Liosa in the eye the next morning as she helped prepare morning supper, wondering if she'd heard her and Artair last night. Her face warmed as she recalled how she'd arched and writhed and moaned beneath Artair, the feel of his hard, muscled body against hers, the torturous pleasure of his lips against her skin.

"I take it ye and my brother enjoyed each other's company last night," Liosa said calmly, dropping a batch of onions into a boiling pot.

Diana nearly chopped off her finger with the knife she was using to dice carrots.

"I—ah—" she stammered, uncertain of how to respond.

"'Tis all right," Liosa said, chuckling. "But I will say this—my brother cares for ye deeply. I can tell. And for that, I'm glad. I've never seen him so taken with a lass as he is with ye."

123

Diana swallowed, uncertain of what to say. She couldn't tell Liosa that nothing could ever truly happen between them because she was leaving soon. A jolt of pain struck her as she realized just how difficult it would be to leave him behind.

She was relieved when Liosa changed the subject, asking her to fetch some spices from the cellar that Keagan and Artair had forgotten to bring up to the kitchens.

Diana didn't see Artair until evening supper, as she divided her time between her room, where she mentally reviewed and practiced spells, and the kitchens where she helped Liosa. But her mind kept returning to thoughts of Artair's masculine beauty, the feel of his body entwined with hers, and by the time evening fell, she ached to see him.

"My brother and Keagan have been working on clearing a path outside—the snow is finally starting to clear," Liosa said, her eyes twinkling as they entered the dining room.

Diana flushed; was her need to see Artair so apparent?

"Here," Liosa continued, smiling warmly as she handed her a platter of freshly baked bread. She seemed to know that Diana needed to do something to occupy herself. "Ye can set the table for supper."

As Diana and Liosa set down plates of bread and stew for supper, Artair and Keagan entered. Keagan greeted his wife with a kiss; Diana's eyes met Artair's, and a firestorm erupted inside her. He offered her a warm smile, one she tried to return with casual politeness. How could she behave normally around him after what they'd shared the night before?

"We saw other men clearing away paths in the distance—it'll likely be safe for ye both tae travel tomorrow or the day after," Keagan said, as they sat down to eat.

"After I escort Diana tae the Highlands, I'm returning tae help ye with the border men," Artair said, focusing on his sister.

Diana lowered her gaze to hide the disappointment that settled over her. The past week had seemed like a haven the snowstorm had forced them into, and now it was back to reality. The journey north to Tairseach, and her eventual departure from Artair.

"Artair—" Liosa began.

"I willnae hear any discord about it, sister. I'm returning with men tae defend yer lands, whether ye want me tae or not," Artair said firmly. "Ye told me ye never turn yer back on family. I'll not turn my back on ye. Were those just words or did ye mean them?"

Surprise—and a flicker of love—flared in Liosa's eyes. She turned to look at Keagan; some agreement seemed to pass between them. Finally, Liosa turned to Artair with a sigh.

"It looks like ye're going tae get yer way, brother," she replied, but offered him a small smile. "I'm not the only stubborn Dalaigh."

Artair returned it, and the tension at the table evaporated.

"Well, since we got through this snowstorm, why donnae we use this meal tae celebrate—considering ye both are soon tae depart? We can have some sweet wine from France—we have it stored in the cellar. We were saving it for Yule, but I think we should enjoy it now."

Artair's smile widened, his face lighting up, and Diana's heart clenched at the sight. His joy was infectious; it struck her then how much she enjoyed seeing him happy.

"That has been the best idea ye've had all week," he said.

"Tell me of yer family, Diana," Liosa said, after Keagan had brought up the wine and poured it for them. "I ken yer parents are gone, but do ye have other family?"

Diana stiffened. There was no suspicion in Liosa's tone, only genuine warmth and curiosity. During their time working together in the kitchens, Diana had only given her brief, vague answers whenever Liosa questioned her about her life and redirected such questions to inquire about Liosa, Keagan and Artair instead.

"My aunt," Diana said, opting to remain as close to the truth as possible. "She lives in England. I have other family in the Highlands—near Tairseach. That's where I was headed when Artair and I met."

"And yer uncle?" Keagan asked, sipping his wine.

"She's a widow," Diana lied. Her aunt Maggie was indeed widowed before Diana had gone to live with her, but Kensa had never been married. For all her interest in guiding people through time to their soul mates, Kensa never seemed concerned with her own love life.

"And yer other kin? The kin ye're meeting in the Highlands?" Liosa asked.

"Cousins I haven't seen for a long time," Diana said, improvising now. "I'm visiting them for Yule."

Keagan seemed satisfied with her response, though she noticed that Liosa's gaze lingered on her for some time. When she looked at Artair, his expression was neutral, though he gave her a subtle nod to indicate she'd improvised well.

Diana had to shove away the guilt she felt over lying to Liosa and Keagan. Even though she'd not spent much time with them, they already felt like close friends—friends she liked very much. They had shattered her preconceived notions about people who lived in the fourteenth century; they were in a warm, loving marriage, and they behaved as each other's equals.

She had to admit to herself that the past wasn't as terrifying as she'd thought. Yes, there had been the scary encounter with Tamhas and his men, but on the whole her time here hadn't been an awful experience.

And, she realized, she had not once yearned for or missed the conveniences of her time—not even when she'd slept in those cold, empty stables with Artair the night they'd shared their first kiss. She'd gotten used to bathing in the basin of fresh rosewater in the mornings before dressing in a comfortable underdress and gown. She enjoyed helping Liosa prepare meals in the kitchens. She looked forward to sitting before the crackling fire with a cup of ale—she'd gotten used to the bitter taste—or sweet wine. It was the type of life she'd envisioned for herself in the manor she was restoring. Only this manor included a gorgeous Highlander and his family whom she genuinely liked.

For the rest of the evening, Diana allowed herself to relax, laughing as Liosa and Artair engaged in telling embarrassing childhood stories about each other. At one point, Liosa got up to demonstrate a dance Artair had performed with two of his friends to impress young women at a castle gathering; Artair corrected her by getting up to pull Diana into his arms.

"No, *this* is how I danced, sister," he said, twirling Diana around.

Diana laughed as he swung her around in his arms to an invisible tune. He suddenly stopped, his blue eyes roaming her face. For several long moments, Diana forgot that Keagan and Liosa were in the room, and it was just the two of them. Artair tightened his grip around her waist, pulling her close, and Diana's lips parted, desire roaring to life inside her.

"I think we'll leave ye both alone."

It was Keagan's wry voice that interrupted them, and Diana started to pull back, her face flaming, but Liosa and Keagan were already heading out of the room, chuckling as they left.

"I think they had the right idea, lass," Artair murmured, and just as he had the night before, he swung her up into his arms and carried her to his chamber.

There, he made love to her until she came with a cry, his name on her lips, and she allowed herself to fantasize—briefly—that she wasn't a time-traveling witch, that she was right where she belonged.

But that fantasy was woefully brief.

She awoke the next morning to the sound of angry shouts outside the manor. She sat up; Artair was already getting dressed, his face white with panic.

"Artair, what's happening?" she asked, panic of her own searing her veins. "Who is that outside?"

"It's Tamhas and his men," he said grimly. "They're here."

CHAPTER 15

*A*rtair tried to keep his breathing steady as he yanked on his clothing.

"Diana, I need ye tae stay here," he said sharply.

"Artair, no. Let me—" she began.

"Diana," he repeated, leveling her with a hard stare and ignoring the look of hurt in her eyes. He would do whatever it took to keep her safe. "Stay. Here."

He hurried out of the chamber, tearing down the stairs, his heartbeat a furious cacophony in his ears. He needed to make certain his sister also stayed out of sight.

He found Keagan in the entry hall, striding toward the door, clutching a sword.

"My sister?" Artair asked.

"I told her tae remain upstairs in our chamber. I'll handle this," Keagan said, moving past him.

"No. *We'll* handle this," Artair said, trailing him to the door.

They opened the door to find Tamhas, Iomhar and several other men outside, seated astride their horses.

Tamhas's eyes widened in surprised recognition at the sight of Artair, before his lips curled in a cruel smile.

"This is a surprise," he said. "We came here tae pay our friends a visit and we find the mysterious Highlander. Where's yer Sassenach?"

"What do ye want?" Artair demanded, ignoring his question as he moved to stand in front of Keagan.

"Laird Padarsan and his lady owe us more of their food stores," Tamhas said, his eyes darting to Keagan. "We're running low after the storm, as are the surrounding farms. But now that ye're here, we'll also take ye and yer bonnie wife—is she here?"

"His whore wife did something tae me," Iomhar sneered, tightening his grip on the reins of his horse, his face turning red with fury. "Bring the bitch tae me."

Rage like Artair had never known before tore through him, and he gripped his dagger, starting toward Iomhar, but the sound of a familiar voice stopped him.

"Artair!"

He froze at the sound of Diana's voice. *No.* He turned, dread coiling around his heart. Both Diana and Liosa now flanked Keagan, who was fruitlessly trying to usher them both back inside.

But Diana stepped past Keagan, glaring at Tamhas and his men.

"Ilsa, get back inside. Ye as well, Liosa," Artair hissed.

"Not until these men leave my property," his stubborn sister said, stepping out to stand next to him, ignoring Keagan's protests.

"Ah. 'Tis heartwarming that ye all ken each other," Tamhas said, looking genuinely delighted by this turn of events. "Since we're all friends, our demands are simple. Domnall and Ilsa—if those are yer names—ye'll come with us. Laird Padarsan and bonnie Liosa, bring us the food we're owed."

"They'll not give ye anything, and we're not coming with ye. Leave these lands at once," Artair snarled.

"I'll make a proposal for ye," Tamhas said, unfazed by Artair's visible rage. "We can leave the food behind—for now. But ye and yer wife will leave with us now, or we come back with five times as many men. When we come back, I willnae be as polite, and we'll take Laird Padarsan and his wife as well."

Artair swallowed, fury and frustration battling within him. He couldn't let them take the others and return with more men. He would die first.

"I'll come with ye—me alone. The women and Laird Padarsan stay behind."

"No." It was Iomhar who spoke up now, his

hungry eyes on Diana. "Ye and yer wife come, or all of ye come."

"No," Artair hissed. "I told ye—"

"Fine," Diana interrupted, stepping forward. "I'll come with you as well."

"Diana, ye'll stay here," Artair ordered, his fear for her making him forget to call her by her false name of Ilsa.

But Diana ignored him, stepping forward with a defiant jut of her chin.

"We'll go with you, but you leave Laird Padarsan and his wife out of this."

"Artair—Diana, no!" Liosa protested from behind them.

"All right," Tamhas said, after exchanging a brief glance with his brother. "Artair and Diana—such lovely names. I wish ye had told me yer true names when we first met. But I'm sure we'll learn much more about ye both."

The smile that curved Tamhas's lips filled Artair with icy dread.

ARTAIR LANDED on his arse as Iomhar tossed him inside an empty storeroom. Iomhar stepped forward, giving him a mocking grin.

"I'm going tae enjoy yer wife—and make her pay for what she did tae me," Iomhar snarled.

Artair scrambled to his feet and charged at him,

but Iomhar slammed the door behind him, and Artair heard the lock turn.

He closed his eyes, sinking against the door, a wave of helplessness washing over him. Tamhas and his men had ridden with them back to Lockerbie and taken them to the same inn they'd stayed in before. But unlike before, it was mostly empty, and the innkeeper seemed terrified of Tamhas and his men—Artair suspected they'd threatened him.

Artair pummeled his fist against the door, frustration tearing through him. He should have locked Diana in his chamber, he should have fought Tamhas and his men—anything to keep her and his family out of harm's way. But he'd done nothing, and now he and Diana were completely at their mercy.

He stepped back from the door, clenching his fists at his sides. As they'd ridden here, Diana had seemed eerily calm, but her face had been pale. Fury seized him; if Iomhar touched Diana, he would kill him. He'd never killed a man, but he could do it easily if it came to protecting Diana.

But he needed to get out of this room first. He took several deep breaths, forcing himself to think. He needed a plan. These men were thieves at their core—they wanted coin and lands. That had to be the only reason they were so interested in him and Diana. He needed to appeal to Tamhas's greed, to make him think he would get what he wanted from them.

By the time Tamhas entered moments later, Artair had put together a hasty plan. He straightened, glowering at him.

"I want tae see my wife," Artair demanded.

"We have much tae discuss first, Artair," Tamhas said, putting an emphasis on his real name. "Tell me, if ye had nothing tae hide, why give us false names?"

"We'd just been robbed by bandits. We didnae trust strangers," Artair said.

"I think ye're still lying tae me," Tamhas said with a sigh. "I'll be honest with ye—I donnae care how ye came tae arrive in an area with no clear roads, with no horses or belongings. Here's what I do care about: I can tell by looking at yer hands and yer clothing that ye're not a poor man. I think ye have lands and coin—and plenty of it tae spare for me and my men. Perhaps ye need motivation tae confirm this for me. I can have Iomhar take yer sweet bonnie Sassenach while ye watch—"

At those words, Artair's carefully constructed plan fell apart. He reacted on instinct, charging toward Tamhas with a roar, his fist colliding with the other man's jaw. Tamhas wasn't prepared for the attack, stumbling back, and Artair leapt onto him, tackling him to the ground. He lifted up Tamhas's head with his hands and slammed it to the ground. Tamhas's eyes rolled back, and he stilled.

Artair stumbled to his feet, his breathing ragged. Never had he used such force on anyone.

He clenched his fists at his sides as he glared down at Tamhas, tempted to keep slamming his head to the floor—but Tamhas was unconscious, though Artair noted that he still breathed. He needed to focus on getting Diana.

He took Tamhas's sword off of his still body and moved to the door, which was now unlocked, peering out. There was no one in the main room except for the innkeeper, who kept his gaze trained on the counter before him, though Artair noticed he was shaking.

He hurried out and approached the innkeeper, who looked up, holding up his hands.

"Please—I donnae want any trouble—" he began.

"I'm not here tae hurt ye. Where are the rest of the men? And the lass who came in with us?"

"They're in front, guarding the door," the innkeeper replied. "The lass is upstairs with the large red-haired man."

Artair turned and crossed the room, darting up the stairs, clutching Tamhas's sword in his hand. He was going to kill Iomhar for even being in the same room as Diana. And if he'd touched her—

He heard a panicked cry at the end of the hall, and terror ripped through him as he rushed toward the sound—to the door at the end of the hall.

He threw it open, stumbling inside.

Diana stood backed up against the far wall, her eyes wild with fear as Iomhar moved toward her, his eyes roaming eagerly over her body.

Artair let out a roar of pure fury and charged forward, his sword outstretched. Iomhar whirled, his eyes going wide with anger of his own as he moved toward Artair.

Artair noticed—too late—that Iomhar clutched a dagger in his hand, raising it to strike as he lunged toward him. Iomhar's dagger was seconds away from piercing him when Iomhar suddenly flew back, striking the wall with such force that his head made a sickening crack, blood pooling from the base of his skull. Iomhar sank to the ground, his eyes wide—and lifeless.

He turned to Diana, who was looking down at her hands, trembling. She'd used her witchcraft, he realized. She'd saved his life.

Artair rushed forward to examine Iomhar, confirming that he was dead before turning to Diana. She was still looking down at her hands, her face pale, her body trembling.

"I—I did that," she whispered. "I killed him."

"Ye had no choice," he assured her. "He would have killed me and raped ye. Tamhas is unconscious downstairs. We have tae leave before the other men return and discover them."

But Diana didn't move.

"Diana, look at me," he murmured. "I ken this was all a great shock tae ye, but we have tae leave before the other men come."

She gave him a dazed nod and allowed him to pull her from the room. Taking her hand, he kept her behind him as they made their way back down to the empty main room. The innkeeper was nowhere to be seen. Artair hoped that he'd fled to safety.

He searched the room and located a back door. Taking a breath, he readied his sword and moved toward it, keeping Diana behind him. But as soon as he threw open the door—several men darted toward them.

He lunged forward, ready to fight—but stopped as he recognized one of the men. Keagan.

"Artair? Diana? Thank God!" Keagan cried, hurrying toward them.

"How are ye here—where are Tamhas's men?" Artair asked, still holding Diana's hand as Keagan ushered them toward a waiting horse.

"Yer sister had me follow ye from a distance. She sent word tae other local farmers—Tamhas and his men have been tormenting all the locals, they were eager tae help. There are a dozen of us—we managed tae scatter Tamhas's men. But we need tae get ye out of here before they bring rein-forcements."

CHAPTER 16

*D*iana was only vaguely aware of her surroundings. Artair's hands on her waist, helping her onto a horse. His arms around her as they rode. His gentle touch as he guided her inside Keagan and Liosa's home.

Her mind was still back in that room in the inn, the memory of it seared onto her mind.

Iomhar had demanded to know—repeatedly—how she'd made him fall asleep during their first encounter.

"Very well," he'd sneered, when she had refused to answer. "I will at least collect on what ye owe me—yer bonnie body. But now I'll make sure ye'll feel no pleasure—the pleasure will only be for me."

Fury and panic had roiled through her, and she'd kicked him in the groin, stumbling back as he let out a howl of pain. She'd cried out as he made his way toward her, silently urging herself to perform a defensive spell, but her mind and body had frozen in terror.

It was only when Artair entered the room that she'd emerged from her panicked haze. She'd seen the dagger in Iomhar's hand as he charged toward Artair, knew that he was only seconds away from killing Artair, and she'd reacted. She didn't know what spell she used; she could only recall a powerful wave of fury and protectiveness sweeping over her, a sizzle of fire beneath her skin.

"Diana."

She looked up, realizing that she was now back in her guest chamber. Artair was gripping her by the shoulders, looking down at her with concern.

"Ye're safe, lass," he murmured. "'Tis over."

He pulled her into his arms, and that was when the dam broke inside of her. She began to weep, and he kept her in his arms as he led her to the bed, where he curled up beside her as she fell into an exhausted sleep.

WHEN SHE AWOKE, it was dark outside, and the bed beside her was empty. She sat up, grogginess still weighing her down. She must have slept for hours. Why she was still so fatigued?

She realized it was her magic that had drained her—Kensa had told her the more powerful the spell, the more taxing it was on the body.

She closed her eyes, shaking as the memory

returned to her. Iomhar approaching her with deadly purpose, then his lifeless eyes as he slid down the wall.

Diana pressed her fingers to her temples. She couldn't let herself dwell on what happened with Iomhar. But even though she knew she'd had no choice but to attack, that he would have killed Artair had she not acted, the guilt lingered.

She stood and made her way out the chamber, heading down the hall. She paused at the top of the stairs; Artair and Liosa's voices carried to where she stood.

"I was the one who killed Iomhar," Artair was saying, and Diana jerked in surprise. "And I knocked Tamhas unconscious," he continued. "They'll send more men here—ye and Keagan cannae stay. Ye need tae find somewhere safe tae go. I'll get myself and Diana north. And then I'm returning with men tae fight them."

"We've been dealing with these men for months. We willnae have them force us out of our home," Liosa snapped.

"Ye have no choice," he barked. "They may kill ye both in retaliation for what I've done."

"If we leave, they'll go after our servants instead," Keagan protested.

"Send them away. They can return after I come back with more men tae defend yer lands."

"We'll come with ye north. We'll not go hide while ye defend our home," Liosa said.

"Liosa, 'tis dangerous—"

"Ye said I'll be part of yer life now, did ye not? I'm not speaking of fighting—I'm no fighter," Liosa continued. "But I can help in other ways, and I'm coming with ye. We both are."

A long silence fell.

"All right," Artair said with a heavy sigh. "Ye're still as stubborn as always, Liosa."

"Aye," Liosa returned. "Ye and me both, brother."

Diana smiled, starting to head down the stairs, but froze at Liosa's next words.

"I can tell ye care about Diana, and I ken ye're lovers. Why are ye so eager tae send her away?" Liosa asked.

"I'm not eager tae send her away. Diana doesnae belong—she doesnae belong with me. She —she has a life of her own. Our run-ins with those men prove 'tis not safe for her here. What's between us—'tis only a brief affair. 'Tis best she goes her own way."

A sharp pain twisted her gut and tears stung her eyes. Swallowing hard, she turned to hurry back to her chamber.

She shook her head, feeling foolish over her reaction. Artair hadn't said anything she didn't already know. So why did it hurt so much?

When he entered her chamber moments later, he had a tray of food. He looked relieved to see that she was awake. She stood stiffly, forcing a polite smile.

"Are ye all right?" he murmured, moving

toward her. He reached out to cup her face, and Diana allowed herself to briefly relish in his touch before stepping back.

"Yes. I was just shaken. I'm fine now."

"I should never have allowed ye tae go with them," he said, his face shadowing with regret.

"No. If I hadn't come, they would have killed you."

Her chest tightened at the thought. Even though guilt lingered over Iomhar's death, she would never regret saving Artair's life.

"Still," he continued, locking his determined blue eyes with hers. "I'm getting ye back tae Tairseach. Liosa and Keagan are traveling north with us, 'tis not safe for them here. I'd rather not travel so soon after a snowstorm, but we've no choice. We'll have tae pray for decent weather as we make our way north," he added, glancing briefly out the window. "And now that yer craft is becoming stronger, perhaps ye can practice transporting yerself back tae yer own time sooner, without the portal. The sooner ye're out of this time, the sooner ye're out of danger."

She tensed at his words, searching his face, but his gaze was steady. *He's right*, she reminded herself. Hadn't she wanted to avoid coming to the past for this very reason—its innate danger?

"Now," he said, "if yer witchcraft has exhausted ye, ye should get more rest after ye eat something. We have a long ride tomorrow—we leave at first light. I want us long gone by the time

Tamhas and his men come looking for vengeance."

He started to leave, but she stopped him.

"Wait," she said, hoping she didn't sound too needy. "Stay. I—I need distraction."

She knew that the moment he left her alone, images of Iomhar and his lifeless eyes would haunt her. Artair seemed to understand, giving her a kind smile.

The meal was a vegetable stew that Liosa had sweetened with honey, and she savored every bite.

"I donnae have many memories of my mother as I was still a bairn when she died, but this is a stew she used tae make for me and Liosa, even though my father insisted she let the castle cook make it," Artair said. "But my mother was stubborn . . . something we both inherited. My mother would tell him, 'My bairns will ken at least one meal directly from their mother.'"

Diana smiled, charmed by the story.

"It sounds like she was quite a woman."

"She was. Many people donnae ken that she was born a commoner. It was quite the scandal when my father, a laird, took her as a wife. But he loved my mother the moment he laid eyes on her."

"My father told me something similar," Diana said, warmed by the memory.

"Aye? How did they meet? Was it during a ritual of some sort?" Artair asked, eyes wide, and Diana laughed.

"Witches don't spend all their time performing

rituals. They met in a mundane way—at universi-ty," she said. "My father told me he had to ask my mother out at least a dozen times before she agreed to date him. She told me she was reluctant to marry a fellow stiuireadh."

"Well, I'm glad she did," Artair said, his voice dropping an octave as his blue eyes settled on her. "Because together, they made the lovely witch sitting across from me."

She flushed, lowering her gaze. Artair stood, reaching out to pull her to her feet.

"Artair—" she said, blinking up at him in surprise.

"I've not thanked ye properly," he murmured, pulling her into his arms, "for saving my life."

He held her close and kissed her, probing her mouth thoroughly with his. She melted into his kiss, and for a few, glorious moments, the trauma of the day faded. She wound her arms around his neck, pressing her body closer to his. She needed more of him. And for as long as she was in this time, she was going to have him.

Diana broke off the kiss and stepped back, lowering her gown. Artair stilled, his Adam's apple bobbing as he swallowed.

"Diana, after what happened today, perhaps ye should—"

"I said I needed a distraction," Diana inter-rupted, arching a brow. "Are you not up to the challenge?"

Artair's expression shifted from concern to mischief, and he gave her a devious smile.

"Oh, I'm up tae the challenge, witch," he whispered.

She let out a moan of delight as he lowered her gown to the floor, lowering his hand to stroke her moist center. Trembling with need, she reached up to pull off his tunic as he stepped out of his kilt, and she ran her hands along every inch of his skin, relishing in the feel of his muscled hardness beneath her fingers.

Keeping her gaze trained on his, she removed his hand from her center and lowered her own hand down to stroke him. He stiffened and let out a strangled moan.

She kept stroking him as she led him back to the bed, pushing him down as she lowered her mouth to his cock, laving the head with her tongue.

"Diana—" he rasped.

She continued to lap at him, luxuriating in the feel of him in her mouth. Artair's body bucked, but he reached down to lift her head from his hardness.

"I want tae come inside ye," he whispered, and pulled her down onto the bed, seizing both of her breasts with his mouth before sinking inside her with a groan.

Diana arched hungrily against him, gasping against his mouth as he began to thrust, their bodies moving together until the pleasure became too much; it coiled like a tight spring within her before bursting, and her orgasm claimed every part of her body. She cried out as he shuddered and came as well, silencing her with a kiss. They both rode out their pleasure until they collapsed together onto the bed.

"Did I distract ye, lass?" he asked, when they'd both caught their breath.

She gave him a teasing smile. "A wee bit."

Her smile faded as she gazed up at his handsome face, reaching up to stroke his firm jaw.

"Artair," she whispered. "I didn't think when Iomhar charged at you with that dagger. I just reacted. All I knew was that I would have done anything to save your life. Anything at all."

His expression softened, and he leaned in to kiss her forehead.

"I would have done the same for ye, my Diana."

She recalled the feeling of power within her as she'd killed Iomhar. For so long she'd resisted her power, but what if she embraced her magic? What if she could do more to help Artair fight Tamhas?

He seemed to read her mind, taking her hand and placing it to his lips.

"I'm getting ye tae Tairseach," he said, and something twisted inside her, her post-coital bliss vanishing. "Away from all this danger—and back tae yer life."

CHAPTER 17

They set out to leave the manor early the next day. They planned to make their first stop in Edinburgh before continuing north to Inverness and then onward to the Highlands. Edinburgh was a two days' ride away, and Inverness another several days' ride. With stops to sleep at inns along the way and to water and feed their horses before changing them in Edinburgh, it would take them a little over a week to arrive in the Highlands.

"A week to get to the Highlands?" Diana had breathed, when he'd detailed their travel plans the night before. "In my time, it would only take a few hours by train. Even less by plane."

"I believe ye, lass, though I donnae ken how 'tis possible," Artair replied, shaking his head.

During his time with Kensa, she'd tried to explain the faster means of transport in the future, but to Artair, such transport sounded dangerous, and Kensa confirmed that many people died in car and plane accidents every year. Artair would trust his horse over any metal contraption, even if it meant getting to his destination took longer.

Artair intended to take Diana to Tairseach before he returned to his manor and sought out the help of the MacGreghor clan. An ache seared his chest at the thought of sending her away, but he had no choice—it was too dangerous for her to stay. And by the time they reached the Highlands, she could leave with a clear heart; she'd done her duty by leading him back to his home and to his time. He would just have to shutter away his pain at her departure and carry the memory of her for the rest of his days: he knew in his heart that no other lass would ever compare to his golden witch.

As they rode away from the manor, his eyes focused on Diana as she rode alongside Liosa. She'd told him her horseback riding skills came from lessons she'd taken as a child in the Scottish countryside with her parents. Besides her riding ability, she'd seemed to adapt to the fourteenth century well.

It relieved him to see that her eyes were no longer shadowed the way they'd been the day before. He hoped that in time she would forget she'd had to kill Iomhar, though he suspected a part of her would always remember. His grip tightened on his reins and his jaw clenched as he recalled the sickening look on Iomhar's face as he'd approached her. Had Diana not killed Iomhar, he would have done it himself.

To calm himself, he focused on the beauty of the waking day around him. The array of colors that filled the sky as the sun rose, the melting snow of the countryside, revealing patches of green earth beneath. The air was brisk and smelled of damp earth. He relished in the cold air on his skin; he had never minded cold weather, and he'd missed the air while he'd been inside Liosa's manor during the storm.

They stopped just before midday to water their horses and eat some of the provisions they'd brought with them. He stood with Keagan as they watched Liosa and Diana speak in hushed tones, sharing a quiet laugh.

"I'm glad my wife and Diana have become friendly. Liosa hasnae had a lady friend for some time. Her days have been filled with matters of the household and the difficulties of getting with child."

"I'm glad as well," Artair said, though a pang pierced him as he spoke the words. Their burgeoning friendship couldn't last; Diana would be leaving soon.

For a brief moment, he allowed himself to imagine Diana staying in this time and continuing her friendship with Liosa, spending her days at his side and filling his empty manor with her infectious light.

But he didn't allow himself to dwell on such thoughts. Diana would be safe—and happy—in her own time. She was too bonnie to stay alone for long; she would find a good man to wed her. Artair himself would find another lass to wed. If Drostan MacGreghor still favored him, he could pair him with another noble's daughter. Yet the thought didn't bring him much comfort, only filling him with jealousy, sadness, and loss.

They continued to ride until they reached the village of Lerick, where they stopped at an inn. The innkeeper recognized Keagan and slapped his shoulder in greeting. After they settled into their rooms, Artair sought out Diana, finding her standing by the window, peering out. Her expression was troubled; he hoped that she wasn't thinking of Iomhar.

Diana needs a respite, he decided. When they arrived in Edinburgh, he would take her around the city, give her a glimpse of city life in this time before she returned to the future. And, selfishly, he knew it would be a way of spending more time with her.

"We're safe here," he said as he entered her room. "There's no need tae fret about anything. I'll not let anything happen tae ye."

"I know," she said, turning to face him, her expression still clouded.

"Then what troubles you?"

She met his gaze, her eyes turbulent. After a moment, she gave him a smile that seemed forced.

"I'm just tired from the day's ride, that's all."

He could tell that she wasn't telling him the

truth. Hurt pierced his chest. After all they'd been through together, he thought she was past hiding things from him. But he told himself that perhaps this was for the best since they were soon to part ways.

He turned away from her, moving to the door.

"I'll see ye downstairs for supper."

DIANA WAS SMILING and laughing with Liosa and Keagan at supper. She'd seemed to set aside whatever had troubled her, though to Artair it seemed as if she was trying too hard to appear relaxed and jovial.

He noticed with irritation that she'd changed from her riding clothes to a crimson gown with a daringly low bodice. He found his eyes, and the eyes of every other man in the inn's dining area—with the exception of Keagan's—on her.

He gritted his teeth, jealousy flooding him as other men eyed his Diana. *Not yer Diana,* he reminded himself. She wasn't his wife. She wasn't even officially his mistress. But that didn't stop anger from roaring to life inside him as she smiled up at the blushing innkeeper who poured more ale into her cup.

"Are ye not cold, lass?" Artair bit out, as the innkeeper scampered away.

She looked at him, raising her eyebrows innocently. "Cold?"

"Aye," he continued. "Given that so much of yer skin is on display."

"Artair," Liosa scolded, but Diana just gave him an easy smile and shrugged.

"Not at all. In fact, I'm quite warm," she said, her eyes glittering with defiance.

"Artair, I ken we discussed this before, but I wanted to ken for certain—how many men do ye think will return with us?" Keagan asked, forcing his gaze away from Diana's distracting bosom.

"I donnae ken. As many who are willing tae make the journey."

"The local farmers are also willing tae help. They may not be fighting men, but Tamhas's men have terrorized them as well, and they want it tae stop," Liosa added.

Keagan reached out to place his hand over Liosa's.

"'Tis all right," he murmured. "We'll reclaim our home, make it safe for us and the locals."

Liosa smiled, leaning in to kiss him. It warmed Artair's heart to see his sister so loved and cared for. But he also felt another unexpected stab of envy at their closeness. His gaze drifted to Diana, who was now focused on her ale.

"I'm going to bed," Diana said abruptly, getting to her feet. "It's been a long day."

"I'll walk ye tae yer room," he said, getting to his feet as well and shooting a warning glare to several men whose eyes eagerly followed Diana's movements.

To his annoyance, Diana looked as if she would protest, but she gave him a reluctant nod, bidding Liosa and Keagan a good night.

After he escorted her to her door, Diana hurried inside.

"Good night, Artair," she said quickly, and closed the door on his face before he could reply.

He stared at the door, stung by her rejection. She'd been acting distant since they arrived.

Did she regret making love to him? Dread coursed through him at the thought. He raised his hand to knock on her door, to demand answers, but he decided against it, dropping his hand to his side.

She doesnae belong in this time, he reminded himself.

Ignoring the shard of pain that pierced his chest, he turned and forced himself to walk away.

CHAPTER 18

*D*iana immediately regretted closing the door on Artair. She forced herself to remain in her room, finally drifting off to sleep with a whirlwind of conflicting emotions. She should have sated her need and desire for him instead of turning him away. Now, she had a need for him that throbbed deep within—and it wasn't just a sexual need. It was an emotional one.

Because she loved him.

She'd never been in love before, not even close, and at first, she'd dismissed her growing feelings for Artair as desire amplified by the mad situation they were in.

But he consumed her thoughts. Her heart lightened whenever he entered the room, and his very presence calmed her. She loved him for his fierce love for his sister. She loved him for his sense of honor, even his stubbornness. She loved him for the lighter parts of himself he seemed to have kept shuttered away—his wicked sense of humor, his laughter, his innate kindness.

She recognized that she loved him in the aftermath of Iomhar's death, when she realized that she'd have killed a hundred men to save his life. Ironically, it was her magic—the force she'd tried to ignore for so long—that made her aware of her love for him. That wave of protectiveness and fury that swept over her at the sight of Iomhar's attempt on his life had propelled the power of her spell. Kensa had told her that magic was entwined with emotions. Her love for Artair had been the force that powered her spell, the force that raced through her with a dizzying sense of power.

She'd mulled over her realization of her feelings for Artair during the ride north, and when Artair had come into her room to check in on her the previous day, it was those thoughts that had raced through her mind.

I love you, she'd wanted to tell him. *I love you, and that terrifies me.*

The thought of leaving him behind no longer filled her with just a pang, or an ache. It filled her with despair. It was a sense of self-preservation that made her shut the door on him.

But avoiding him wouldn't keep her powerful emotions at bay. Nothing could. Not even the abyss of time that would soon separate them.

As they rode away from the inn the next morning, a shard of grief tore through her at the thought. In her own time, Artair would be long dead. As would Liosa, with her fierce spirit. Keagan, with his inherent kindness and the burning love he had for his wife.

Tears sprung to her eyes, but she forced herself to blink them back, to focus on guiding her horse down the muddy, well-trodden road that led out of the village. It relieved her that Artair rode a few yards ahead with Keagan. But Liosa rode at her side, her perceptive gaze trained on her face.

When they stopped for their first rest break, Liosa approached her with a concerned frown.

"Are ye all right, Diana?" she asked. "Ye've been pale and quiet since we left the inn."

"I'm fine," Diana said quickly. Too quickly.

Liosa arched a skeptical brow, glancing back at Artair and Keagan. They stood yards away, out of earshot, tending to their horses. Liosa stepped closer, lowering her voice.

"If ye're sad over having tae leave Artair . . . then perhaps ye shouldnae."

Diana stared at her. "What?"

"My brother loves ye. We may have been apart for long, but I still ken him. And I can tell by the way he looks at ye. 'Tis not common for him tae open his heart. If ye leave him behind, I fear he will become the shuttered and closed off man I left behind all those years ago. I think ye're good for him, Diana."

Diana's heart picked up its pace. She badly wanted Liosa's words to be true, but they weren't. She knew beyond a shadow of a doubt that Artair desired her, that he cared about her, but love? If he loved her, *he* would have been the one to suggest that she stay. Instead, he seemed determined to send her away.

"Artair desires me, that's all," Diana said. "And —I can't stay."

"Why not?" Liosa challenged. "What's waiting for ye back in England?"

Modern conveniences. My job. My old life. She tried to summon up some enthusiasm for those things, but none held any appeal for Diana. If she was truly honest with herself, she'd become a solicitor simply as a means of getting a job that was as from magic as possible.

Relief filled her when Keagan called for them, saving her from having to answer the question.

This time, she rode a few paces behind Liosa, avoiding her lingering looks. For all of Liosa's attention, Artair didn't pay her any mind at all, speaking only to Liosa and Keagan as they rode. She wondered with a sharp pang if he was taking her distance a step further and conversing with her as little as possible until it came time for them to part ways.

When they finally arrived in Edinburgh, some of her tension dissipated; now there was something else for her to focus on. Diana took in Edinburgh as they approached, awe coursing through her. It was certainly not the Edinburgh of the twenty-first century—it was much smaller, more like a large village than a city, surrounded by massive city walls that were long gone in her time. She could see Edinburgh Castle perched on the same hilltop crag —Castle Rock—that it rested upon in her time, though like Edinburgh itself, it was smaller.

They entered Edinburgh through one of the open gates along the southern wall, and Diana took in the patchwork of narrow closes and wynds, the markets, homes and shops, the residents bustling to and fro. The houses ranged from simple cottages to finer merchants' homes. The stench of refuse and sewage hit her nostrils, as did the succulent smell of roasting meats from taverns they passed. Church bells sounded in the distance along with the shouts of laborers and the hum of conversation of passersby. Around them, packhorses stockpiled with vegetables and grain made their way toward the markets.

They came to a stop at an inn in central Edinburgh, one that was larger than the other inns they'd stayed in so far, filled with many more travelers. She heard both Lowland and Highland accents, along with English and Norse.

When they'd paid for their rooms and escaped the bustle of the other guests, Artair fell into step beside her as they headed upstairs to their rooms.

"Would ye like for me tae escort ye around Edinburgh tomorrow? We plan tae stay for a day tae change horses before we make our way north tae Inverness. I thought ye'd want tae see more of the fourteenth century than just muddy roads and inns."

Delight rippled through her at his words. Though she was curious about what Edinburgh was like in this time, she mostly wanted to spend more time with Artair.

"I would love to."

WHEN DIANA and Artair headed out the next morning, Liosa and Keagan opted to remain behind, telling them they wanted to rest at the inn but urged them to enjoy themselves. By the twinkle in Liosa's eyes, Diana suspected that they were giving them alone time on purpose.

They made their way through the narrow streets to St. Giles Cathedral, which he called the "High Kirk of Edinburgh." She could tell that it was partially burnt and in the process of reconstruction; Artair told her that a fire had torn through it several years ago. His eyes widened in surprise when she told him that the cathedral still existed in her time.

This became a bit of a game between them, with Artair pointing out certain landmarks and Diana telling him whether it existed in the future. It didn't surprise him that Edinburgh Castle still existed, but he did seem surprised to learn that Nor Loch, at the base of Castle Rock, would eventually get drained and become a public park.

Artair reached for her hand as he led her down the wynds of St. Mary's and Blackfriars. A shiver of excitement roiled through her at his touch; she had to concentrate as she told him that these wynds would eventually get demolished and become wider streets. They soon made their way through the bustling markets of Grassmarket and Cowgate, both of which existed in her time—but as neighborhoods rather than markets.

"It sounds like Edinburgh of the future hasnae changed much," Artair mused as they headed away from Cowgate and back to the inn.

"The older part—this part—of Edinburgh becomes a neighborhood called Old Town. Much of the city's historical character has been preserved. It's popular with tourists."

"Tourists?" Artair asked with a baffled frown.

"Someone who travels to a destination for a holiday. It's like—what we're doing right now. In this time, only royalty and the wealthy travel for pleasure. Traveling is easier for the common people in my time."

"Ah," he said, nodding with understanding as they stepped aside to allow a horse-drawn cart to pass by. "It seems like things have changed for the better in the future, from all that ye told me. We'll have tae make certain tae get ye back tae it."

His tone was light, but his words pierced her with hurt. She set it aside to face him.

"Artair," she said. "I'm sorry. For my distance yesterday."

"'Tis all right," he assured her, though she noted the relief that filled his face. "Are ye all right?"

I love you.

165

"Yes," she said, forcing a smile. "It's just . . . everything that's happened has been so overwhelming."

"I understand," he said, reaching out to pull her into his arms. "I say we only focus on enjoying each other and our time together while we can."

While we can, Diana thought, a painful ache searing her chest. But she gave him a bright smile.

"All right," she replied.

He surprised her by placing his hand on her nape and pulling her in for a kiss, right there on the street.

After a startled beat, Diana responded, wrapping her arms around him, not caring who was watching. He released her, his breathing ragged with desire, before taking her hand and leading her inside the inn, barely breaking stride as he took her to her room. He closed the door behind them and pressed her against the wall, his eyes roaming over her face.

"I donnae intend tae just make love tae ye. I enjoy yer company; today was nothing but joy for me. But I'll not lie, lass. 'Tis hard tae be around ye and not want tae touch this skin," he growled, reaching out to lower her bodice and capturing a taut nipple in his mouth. "Tae not taste this sweetness . . . "

Diana's body quaked with anticipation and need as he hiked up her gown, sinking to his knees before her. She gasped as he snaked his tongue inside her, moaning with pleasure.

"Artair . . . " she whispered, tendrils of pleasure coiling around every part of her body.

"Ye may have the power of witchcraft, but ye donnae ken the power ye have over me, my golden witch," he whispered, removing his tongue from her center and standing.

He maneuvered her back to the bed, stripping her of her gown and himself of his clothing as they moved.

Diana took control, straddling him when they reached the bed. Keeping her eyes locked on his, she sank down onto his hardness, throwing her head back with pleasure as he gripped her breasts and they began to move together. When their pleasure reached a mutual crescendo, and they shuddered together in climax, she thought the words she couldn't allow herself to say.

I love you, Artair.

CHAPTER 19

*A*fter their night together in Edinburgh, Artair realized that something had shifted in his relationship with Diana. There was a closeness, an intimacy that hadn't been there before. Perhaps it was the knowledge that they should savor each moment they had together and no longer deny their intense attraction.

Now, during their days of riding, he rode at her side, pointing out natural landmarks which he was familiar with, and Diana would tell him if it was still there in her time—though she told him that much of Scotland's countryside had changed little over the centuries.

To his relief, it didn't snow during their days of riding, but it did rain, forcing them to seek out shelter for the night in the nearest inn they could find.

Whenever they stopped to rest, eat or water the horses, he and Diana would find a tucked away loch or grove and walk along it, their hands entwined, sharing passionate kisses he had to force himself to end for fear of taking her right there in the open.

His sister and Keagan seemed pleased by their open intimacy, often riding ahead to give them privacy, or politely telling them they were going to water their horses a few yards away to give them alone time together. For this he was grateful, not just because he wanted as much time with Diana as possible, but because he didn't want his sister to overhear them discussing Diana's witchcraft or the future.

During the nights, they thoroughly explored each other's bodies. Artair couldn't get enough of her; every time he made love to her, he only wanted her more.

He learned how to work every inch of her body —to the spot at the base of her throat that he would nip at, causing her to whimper, her rosy nipples that he loved to suckle, to the taste of her sweet quim as he feasted upon her until she moaned and quivered her release.

But there were other aspects of their nights together that he enjoyed as well. He loved watching her sleep. She slept like a lad, with her arms and legs spread, her mouth open, and snores erupting from her lovely lips. Her face flamed and she gave him a playful shove when he told her how she slept.

What he enjoyed most about their nights was

the feel of her in his arms after they made love. Her softness as he held her close to his chest, a multitude of emotions churning within him as he felt her heart pounding in tandem with his own, relishing in how right she felt in his arms.

The day before they reached Inverness, they stopped on the outskirts of a small patch of forest to water their horses by a stream and eat their food stores. After he tied up his and Diana's horses, they made their way into the forest, finding a small grove.

"Sometimes my parents would drive me to Scotland and take me to old groves like these where druids used to practice their rituals," Diana said, as they walked hand in hand. "They would show me simple spells and I remember feeling such . . . awe."

"Show me one," he said, turning to face her.

He knew that she practiced spells whenever she had an idle moment, usually after supper at whichever inn they were staying at, when he lingered behind to converse with Liosa and Keagan. There had been times when he'd entered their room to find her murmuring a spell beneath her breath as she used her magic to light a candle or open a window or door. He would lean back against the door, just taking her in with quiet awe. She seemed increasingly comfortable with her magic, with who she was and what she was capable of as a witch.

Now, Diana bit her lip, looking around the grove. She moved a few steps ahead and knelt down to the ground, covered in early winter's frost, and held out her hand.

He watched in amazement as a wildflower bloomed, its yellow petals incongruously bright amid the darker forest plants and soil.

"I cannae believe ye didnae use yer witchcraft in yer own time, lass," he murmured. "Tis a gift."

"I'm starting to realize that now," she said, straightening. "It was grief and pain that made me turn my back on it. But . . . I'm more open to it now. I don't know how I'll go back to being a regular solicitor when I return."

Her return. To the future. It was unspoken between them, but the closer they got to Inverness, the closer they got to Tairseach—to going their separate ways. He swallowed, forcing a smile as he reached out to take her hand.

"We should get back."

"Let me try one more," Diana said, turning back to face the grove. "You might want to stand back for this."

Artair took a cautious step back, and Diana raised her hands. He watched as she closed her eyes, murmuring the words of a spell in Latin.

"*Constitue super terram duris dolor ossibus ardet.*"

A ripple of heat seared the air around him, and his eyes widened as a part of the grove caught flame.

"Diana!" he shouted, panic surging through him.

Diana's eyes flew open. She hastily uttered the words of another spell, and a rush of wind snuffed out the flames.

She turned to him with an apologetic smile, looking surprised by her own power. But her smile faltered as her gaze fell on something behind him. He stiffened, turning to follow her gaze—and his heart leapt into his throat.

Liosa and Keagan stood there, their eyes wide, their mouths agape. Liosa sunk to her knees, pressing her hands to her mouth.

"My God," she whispered. "Ye're a witch."

MOMENTS LATER, Artair and Diana stood before Liosa, who paced back and forth, shaking her head as if trying to shake what she had just seen out of her mind. Keagan leaned against a tree, silent and pale.

After Liosa and Keagan had discovered them, Diana had given him a subtle nod, and he knew he had her permission to tell his sister and brother-in-law—everything.

And so, he told them. Everything. From his vanishing through time, to the existence of stiuireadh, to Diana assisting him back through time. He wasn't certain how his sister would take all this—if she would even believe it—but he hoped that her affection toward Diana would make her set aside any fear or anger. He was less certain of

Keagan, but he suspected his wife's reaction would influence his feelings.

"Tairseach," Liosa said suddenly, stopping to face them both. "You said the portal is at Tairseach? And that's why ye're going back there?"

"Aye," Artair said.

"I kent that place sounded familiar. When I was a girl, I remember hearing rumors about it. About people disappearing. But my maids always told me it was nonsense."

"People do disappear there. But they disappear through time. Liosa, I wouldnae believe any of this myself had it not happened tae me, but I hope—"

"There's no need to convince me," Liosa interrupted, holding up her hand. "I believe ye. How can I not? I just saw Diana conjure fire with my own eyes. 'Tis not much of a leap tae assume she can travel through time. I just cannae—" She trailed off, shaking her head again. "Magic. Traveling through time. Sounds like a bedtime tale one would tell their bairns."

"I ken," he said. "I can hardly believe it myself."

Liosa swallowed, finally looking at Diana.

"Ye used yer witchcraft tae bring my brother back tae his own time. And when ye were both held hostage . . . ye saved his life using it?"

Diana expelled a breath and gave her a shaky nod. "Yes."

Liosa closed her eyes, and when she opened them, they were awash with tears.

"Then I have only tae thank ye."

A powerful wave of relief washed over him as Liosa approached Diana, pulling her into her arms in a warm embrace.

"Thank ye for bringing my brother back tae me," she whispered.

She released Diana, who also looked relieved—and surprised. Liosa moved over to Artair and gave him a ferocious glare.

"Diana gets an embrace and I get a look like that?" he asked, raising his eyebrows.

"Aye. For not telling me any of this sooner. I kent something was odd about Diana. 'Tis why I was harsh with her and didnae trust her before. I kent she was hiding something, but I can also tell she has a good heart and cares for ye. Ye, brother, should have trusted me from the start."

"Aye?" Artair challenged. "If I'd told ye that Diana was a time-traveling witch, after I'd not seen ye for so many years—ye'd have believed me?"

"Aye," Liosa returned fiercely. "It may have taken me a few moments tae accept, but we're family. Sharing things, even things like this, are part of being in a family. I need ye tae trust me going forward if we're tae be in each other's lives."

"I do," he said, holding his sister's gaze. "And I will."

"Good," Liosa said, turning to Diana. "And I trust ye, Diana. Ye've earned it on account of yer good heart—and by saving my brother's life."

CHAPTER 20

*N*ow that Liosa and Keagan knew Diana's true identity, a weight had been lifted from her shoulders. After what happened to her parents, she'd feared what people in the past would do if they learned she was a witch. But Liosa and Keagan weren't random people, they were Artair's family, and they accepted her, which meant more to her than she'd realized.

After they recovered from their shock, Keagan and Liosa peppered her with questions as they continued north. What was her time like? What was it like traveling through time? How did her magic work?

She'd thought answering such questions would be tiresome, especially considering Artair had asked many of the same, but it was a relief to openly discuss her magic. As she answered each question, Liosa and Keagan looked at her with

177

increasing mystification and awe; it became difficult to keep a straight face.

But Artair didn't look amused.

"Diana may be a witch, but she's still the same lass ye've kent," he said with annoyance. "And be certain tae keep Diana's true identity tae yerselves. Donnae speak of it outside our group."

Liosa scowled. "Do ye think I'm a fool, Artair? Of course we willnae. But we will continue tae ask questions."

"As long as ye do it when we're alone," Artair said, giving her a sharp look.

As soon as they arrived at the inn in Inverness, Liosa entered her room while the men were settling the horses.

"Ye can help us," Liosa said. "We have tae fight off Tamhas and his men when we return tae our home. But with yer witchcraft—"

"I'm returning to Tairseach," Diana interrupted. "And I can't practice magic openly. It's too risky."

"I ken there's something ye can do tae help. Ye've already used yer magic tae save Artair's life," Liosa insisted.

Diana expelled a breath. She had already considered this possibility on her own. But she didn't know how she could use her magic to help without exposing herself—and therefore putting Artair and his family at risk for harboring a witch. Just because Liosa and Keagan had accepted what she was didn't mean anyone else would.

"I think Artair's men will do just fine," she said, ignoring the uncertainty that roiled through her. "And—I have to get back to my own time. That's where I belong."

"You donnae believe that."

"Yes, I do," Diana insisted, though there was no conviction behind her words. "I care about your brother, but I have to leave. I—I don't want to discuss this anymore."

Liosa held up her hands, giving her a look of apology.

"I'm sorry. Keagan tells me I can be insistent. But . . . think about what I've said, Diana."

Liosa left her alone, and Diana sank down onto her bed with a wary sigh.

She *could* help them fight Tamhas and his men by performing subtle magic in ways most wouldn't notice. A Concealing spell to hide the number of men they had, making it seem like Tamhas could easily defeat them. Defensive spells to shield bystanders from harm. A spell here and there that could add up to turn the tide in Artair's favor. What better way to ensure Artair's safety before she returned to her own time? And she'd have more time with the man she loved.

By the time she joined the others for supper, her doubts had dissipated, and Liosa's suggestion had taken root in her mind.

"What's on yer mind, lass?" Artair asked, taking a swig of his ale.

Diana could feel Liosa's gaze burning into her skin. That gave her the confidence she needed.

"I was just thinking that . . . maybe I can stay longer. To help with the fight against Tamhas."

Liosa grinned, pleasure flickering across her face, while Keagan raised his eyebrows with surprise. Artair, however, tensed and glowered at her.

"No," he growled. "Ye were nearly raped and killed by those bastards. Ye're not going anywhere near them again. I'm taking ye tae Tairseach."

Diana glared at him, clenching her fists at her sides. She'd forgotten how obstinate Artair could be.

"You didn't even ask how I could—"

"I donnae care *how*," Artair snapped. "I willnae let ye put yerself in danger, Diana. I'll hear no more of it."

Diana swallowed hard, hurt and anger swirling through her. If he cared about her, he would see her as more than just a body to warm his bed at night. More than just a delicate flower whom he needed to protect. Had she not taken them both back through time? Had she not saved his life? But he wouldn't even consider allowing her to help, knowing what power she possessed.

"I've lost my appetite," she bit out, getting to her feet.

He returned her glare. "As have I."

"Brother," Liosa said tentatively. "Perhaps ye should listen tae—"

"Was this yer idea, Liosa?" he demanded. "Putting foolish notions in Diana's head?"

"Donnae raise yer voice tae my wife," Keagan snapped.

"Yer wife is trying tae get Diana killed."

"*Diana* is standing right here," Diana interrupted, tired of him speaking about her as if she weren't there. "You are a stubborn prat, Artair Dalaigh. You can't tell me whether or not I can help. I choose to help—and not just for you, but for your sister and Keagan, who I care about. You can throw a tantrum if you'd like, but you can't stop me."

He stood, towering over her. He was so close that she could feel his body heat seeping into her skin. Hot desire ricocheted throughout her body and she felt a hint of moisture between her thighs. It irritated her that she could be so furious with him—and so inflamed with lust—at the same time.

"Oh, I can, lass," he seethed. "I'll tie ye up myself and throw ye over my shoulder if I have tae."

Diana gave him a glittering smile that she hoped looked dangerous.

"You've only seen a glimpse of what I'm capable of," she said, keeping her voice low.

Artair's eyes narrowed.

"Are ye threatening me, lass?"

"All right," Keagan said with a sigh, clambering to his feet to move in between them. "We're all tired from riding all day. I think we all should take a break, get some rest, and then we can—"

"There's no need," Artair said, still glaring down at Diana. "I'll retire tae my own room."

With one last glare at Diana, he turned to stalk away. Diana watched him go, her anger dissipating, giving way to her lingering hurt. Liosa stood and touched her arm.

"'Tis all right," she assured her. "He just needs time tae calm down."

But the stalemate continued. Artair removed his things from their shared room and purchased his own room for the night. For the first time in several nights she slept alone.

As she lay alone in her bed that night, she had to fight her need for him—and her anger—as she stared up at the ceiling.

Did he really think that giving her the cold shoulder would change her mind? If anything, she was now more determined to stay and help with the fight. If he thought she would back down from this because he threw a tantrum, he was sorely mistaken.

With defiance—and hurt—still roiling through her, Diana allowed her growing fatigue to claim her.

Diana awoke in the middle of the night, her heart

hammering, knowing in her gut that *something was very wrong*.

She lay still, her mouth dry, listening to the silence. After several long moments, she heard horse hooves approaching the inn and without having to look out the window . . . she knew.

Tamhas and his men had found them.

She moved quickly, putting a gown on over her underdress and stepping out into the hall. Artair was already there, his hand on the hilt of his sword. She straightened; now was the time to put their differences aside.

"I need you to trust me," she whispered. "I need you to get your sister and Keagan and bring them to my room. Bring all of your belongings. *Please.*"

He hesitated for only a moment before obliging. She returned to her room, praying that the spell she had in mind would work.

Moments later, Liosa and Keagan rushed inside, followed by Artair. She closed the door to her room, her heart leaping into her throat as she heard the shouts of men downstairs.

Diana looked at her door, swallowing as she pressed her hands to it.

"Cruthaich an t-seòmar seo bho shealladh daonna. Cruthaich an t-seòmar seo bho shùilean daonna."

She murmured the words of the spell, over and over, until her hands warmed as she felt her magic

183

responding to her command. Finally, she stepped back, turning to look at Artair and the others.

"No matter what you hear," she whispered. "Remain silent."

They were all pale, but they nodded.

Diana turned back to the door, her body tense as she waited. She heard more shouts, and footsteps pounding up the stairs. Tamhas's unmistakable voice sounded down the hall, along with several others.

Doors slammed open, and she heard angry cries and protests from the other guests. The footsteps approached her door, and Diana's heart hammered against her rib cage. *Trust your magic,* her father had once told her. And so, she did, standing in tense silence even as she heard a man's harsh breathing only centimeters away on the other side of the door.

It seemed like an eternity before the footsteps retreated. Diana turned, moving past the others to look out the window.

Tamhas and his men mounted their horses, casting one last glance back at the inn before riding away until he and his men vanished from view.

And only then did Diana allow herself to breathe.

CHAPTER 21

"What did ye do?" Keagan asked Diana, his voice filled with awe. "Why didnae they come in?"

"I used a Concealing spell," Diana said. "To Tamhas and his men, the door just looked like a wall. They couldn't tell we were in here."

"Christ," Keagan said, shaking his head in amazement. "Ye saved our skins, Diana."

She gave him a weak smile, but she still looked shaken.

Artair moved over to her, cupping her face with his hands.

"Diana," he whispered, shame filling him. "My golden witch. Once again . . . I was a fool."

She met his eyes briefly before moving away from him without a word. He felt Liosa and Keagan's eyes on him and swallowed hard, deciding to remain silent for now. Diana was still upset with him for doubting her, and he couldn't blame her.

They remained in Diana's room for some time after Tamhas and his men rode way. Artair stood by the door, next to Diana, his hand on the hilt of his sword in case the men returned.

"We should leave now—not wait 'til first light," Artair said finally, turning to face the others. "They may return then."

The others nodded in agreement. His eyes fell on Diana, who still looked pale from the effort of performing her spell. Awe coursed through him; the witchcraft she'd used to save them had been . . . miraculous. She'd proven how wrong he was about sending her away, and how right she was about staying to help.

Regret twisted his gut as he recalled the harsh words they'd shared, at how foolishly angry he'd been—so angry he'd deprived himself of her beautiful body for the night.

But icy fear had seized him when she'd suggested helping. He could only see her terrified face as Iomhar approached her and imagined what Tamhas would do to her if he ever caught her. His protectiveness had made him dismiss her, even though he knew that she was strong and more than capable of holding her own.

He tried to meet her eyes, to communicate how sorry he was with a look, but she avoided his gaze. When they were away from the inn, he'd have to pull her aside and apologize.

His hand tightened on the hilt of his sword as his thoughts turned to Tamhas. How had the bastard found them? It chilled him to the bone that he'd tracked them this far north. But as much of a bastard as Tamhas was, Artair could glean the other man's intelligence. Tamhas knew Artair was from the Highlands. Perhaps he'd tormented some local to tell him that Artair and the others had fled to the Highlands to get more men to fight. Most travelers stopped in Inverness before continuing on to the Highlands, and there were few inns in Inverness. It wouldn't have been too difficult to conclude that they may be here.

His body tensed with dread. It was quite possible that Tamhas had been on their trail the entire time. While he'd been making love to Diana, holding her hand as they walked through sunlit groves and lochs, Tamhas had narrowed in on them. It was another reason he'd wanted to send Diana away; she was a distraction.

But it was too late for that. Even if he did send Diana away, she'd already burrowed herself into his heart, into his soul: she would consume his thoughts no matter what.

They waited for more time to pass before making their way out of the inn, using its rear door.

After fetching their horses from the stables, they rode due west instead of north at Artair's insistence—north was where Tamhas would expect them to go.

They stopped to water their horses just as the sun rose above the horizon. He used the opportunity to pull Diana aside.

"I'm not going back to Tairseach until these men are dealt with," she said fiercely, her body stiffening at his touch. "I just proved—again—that—"

"I'm not going tae tell ye tae leave," he interrupted. "I want tae apologize—and tae thank ye for saving us. Ye have proved how invaluable ye are."

She looked surprised at this, her mouth falling shut. She'd been prepared for a fight.

"Ye were right," he continued with a sigh. "I was behaving like an overprotective fool. Ye have tae ken how much I care for ye, lass. I still think of my fear when ye were alone with Iomhar, how I was helpless tae protect ye. But I never should have doubted what ye're capable of," he murmured, reaching out to pull her close.

It relieved him that she didn't resist, relaxing into his arms. He buried his face in her hair.

"Ye amaze me, Diana. My witch."

Diana pulled back slightly, her face lighting up with a lovely smile. She reached up to wind her arms around his neck.

"And don't you forget how amazing I am, you stubborn Scot."

He returned her smile as she pressed her lips to his. They kissed fervently, not caring that they were in full view of Liosa and Keagan.

"Ye're making me and my husband look like we donnae care for each other, the way ye two are mooning about," Liosa said with a groan.

They broke apart, a warm flush spreading

across Diana's cheeks, but Artair held onto her hand as he gave his sister a teasing, defiant smile.

"Then perhaps ye should show yer husband more affection, sister," he said.

They all shared a laugh, needing a moment of levity after the danger they'd barely escaped.

As they continued riding into the familiar surroundings of the Highlands, with its expansive glens, lochs that glittered beneath the rising sun, the hazy outline of snowcapped mountains in the distance, his unease returned. If Tamhas had tracked them this far north, he could possibly find out where he lived, what clan he was affiliated with.

He tried to quell his fear, to tell himself that the Highlands were massive, filled with unfamiliar terrain for someone from the Lowlands. Even if Tamhas could track him down, it would take time. But his fear remained.

They soon arrived at another village, one he'd stayed at several times in the past when he'd traveled south. It would be their final stop before making their way to the lands of Clan MacGreghor where they would ask Drostan MacGreghor for reinforcements, before returning to Artair's manor.

"I'll need tae make certain Tamhas and his men arenae there first," he said, eyeing the inn as they approached. It was unlikely that Tamhas was there, but after last night he wanted to be certain.

"I'll come too," Diana said.

It was on the tip of his tongue to protest, and

Diana gave him a challenging look. He reminded himself that he needed to prove he was true to his word and would allow her to help.

He nodded, and together they rode ahead.

The inn was mostly empty with only a few patrons nursing cups of ale. The innkeeper told him that no one matching Tamhas's description had been there. Only then did Artair pay for their rooms for the night.

As they ate a supper of smoked cod and bread, they spoke quietly of their plans going forward.

"Now I'm thinking that Tamhas tracking us this far north is good. Here, I have the advantage of my connection tae Clan MacGreghor—and tae my own men."

"Aye," Keagan said, "but Tamhas is no fool. He'd not attack without men. If I was Tamhas, I'd seek out rival clans tae help me. We need tae plan on him doing such a thing."

"Ye're right," Artair said. "After I get men tae help us fight, I need tae lure Tamhas tae me. We'll have tae spread word that I'm back at my manor, that I've bragged about killing a border man by the name of Iomhar."

"No," Diana protested. "Artair—"

"'Tis his anger over Iomhar's murder that has driven him tae the Highlands, I ken it," he interrupted. "We need tae use it tae our benefit. Get him tae come tae us. Inciting his anger further is the best way tae keep him in the Highlands."

Liosa and Keagan nodded their agreement, but

Diana said nothing, picking at her food. She remained silent for the rest of the meal, and when he trailed her into the room they would share for the night, he turned her to face him.

"What's the matter, lass?"

"I'm frightened for you," she whispered. "I'm the one who killed Iomhar, but you're putting a target on your back."

"'Tis necessary," he said firmly. "I will happily take his focus off of ye. I'll not let him harm ye again."

"You agreed to let me help!"

"I did. I will," he returned. "But I'm going tae do everything I can tae keep the fight between me and Tamhas. The more focused he is on me, the less he is on ye, my sister and Keagan."

Diana's face was still a storm of conflict. He moved close to her, bending down to swing her up into his arms. She gasped with surprise.

"I donnae doubt yer power, yer strength," he whispered, lowering her lovely body to the bed. "But ye cannae ask me tae not try and protect ye."

Her breath hitched as he reached down to lift her gown, keeping his gaze locked on hers. He leaned down to kiss her, thoroughly exploring the depths of her mouth with his tongue as he continued to hitch up her gown.

"Artair," she moaned, as he tested her readiness by dipping a finger inside her. He gave her a wicked smile. She was soaking wet for him.

"I ken ye'll do everything in yer power tae

protect me. I havenae forgotten what ye've done tae save my hide. But Diana, ye're also mine tae protect, as I've been yers. Mine. Do ye understand?"

He didn't wait for her response, lifting his kilt to sink inside her.

Diana gasped as he began to move, clenching his teeth at the pleasurable feel of her tightness clamped around him.

"Diana," he rasped. "Do ye understand?"

She didn't respond, whimpering as he continued to thrust inside her. He paused, and she let out a cry of protest.

"Please, Artair," she whispered.

"Answer me," he growled, nipping the base of her throat.

"I understand," she whispered. "I'm yours to protect. As you're mine."

"Aye," he grunted his agreement as he again began to thrust, his eyes trained on her lovely face, wanting to take in every moment of her pleasure. "Mine."

And he came with a roar as she shuddered beneath him, his protectiveness, his possessiveness, and his desire for her roiling together as one. *Mine.*

THEY RODE out just after first light. Artair continually searched their surroundings to make certain that no one followed them as they rode, but other than a few stray riders he could make out in the distance, he saw no one that seemed to pose a threat.

Whenever his gaze met Diana's, a flush spread across her face. He knew she was thinking of their night together, of his possessive words. It took much effort for him to concentrate on riding, to not revel in the memory of her writhing beneath him, her cry as she fell apart beneath him, the satisfaction that raced through him as she'd agreed that she was his to protect—as he was hers.

His thoughts were still filled with their night together when they approached MacGreghor Castle several hours later, just before midday. He took it in, a tumult of emotions washing over him. He'd been a different person the last time he was here, prepared to do his duty and marry Caitria, to confine himself to a life without love or passion.

His gaze strayed to Diana. Now he struggled to imagine such a life.

He kicked the sides of his horse to speed up and ride ahead of the others. He could only pray that Drostan and the other clan nobles weren't angry with him for his disappearance, that they would believe the false tale he would tell them. It was crucial that Drostan believed him if he was going to spare his men to help Artair fight Tamhas.

As they drew closer to the front gates of the castle, panic coursed through him at the sight of two riders riding toward them from the distance. Instinctively, his hand went to the hilt of his sword and he guided his horse to block his sister and Diana.

But he stilled when the two figures came into view. One was Caitria, her eyes wide with astonishment as she took him in. The other man . . . looked exactly like him.

It was Niall O'Kean.

CHAPTER 22

*E*very eye in the great hall rested on Artair as he stood opposite Laird Drostan MacGreghor and his wife Lady MacGreghor. Niall and Caitria sat next to them, along with several other clan nobles.

Diana stood behind Artair, along with Liosa and Keagan, trying not to stare at Niall. The resemblance between him and Artair was striking, it was easy to see how he'd passed for Artair. But there were subtle differences. Artair's hair was longer, his eyes a slightly darker shade of blue. And most importantly, she didn't feel the hot rush of desire that coursed through her whenever her eyes landed on him.

Niall had given her a cursory look as he'd led them into the castle, but his focus was mostly on the lovely red-haired woman at his side, Caitria.

Jealousy had filled her at the sight of the woman Artair had almost wed. She was beautiful—

and younger—than she was, with flowing red hair and bright green eyes.

Genuine delight had entered Caitria's eyes at the sight of Artair, and Diana had felt the possessive urge to put her hand on Artair's arm. But as soon as Caitria's eyes had returned to Niall, Diana relaxed, as the look she gave Niall was infused with love. With that one look, Diana knew, without any doubt, that Caitria's heart belonged only to Niall.

They'd only spoken briefly to Niall and Caitria before they'd brought them to the great hall. When Artair told Niall that Diana was a time traveler, and he'd returned to this time from the future, they agreed they had much to discuss—and would talk more in private.

When they entered the great hall to meet Laird MacGreghor, a tall and broad-shouldered man with dark hair and warm brown eyes, he and his wife had gone pale with shock. Artair had told Laird MacGreghor the false story he'd rehearsed with Kensa explaining his absence.

"Shortly after I arrived at yer castle, I decided tae go on a ride. I went farther than I intended and fell from my horse. A lad came upon me and took me tae a nearby healer—she tended tae me during the weeks I was in my false sleep," Artair said.

Now, Laird MacGreghor stared at Artair, his face pale with shock.

"How did ye end up all the way at the border?" he asked.

"I'm Artair's sister; I sent a rider north tae

search for him," Liosa interjected before Artair could reply, stepping forward. "I ken the healer who took care of him, she kent of our family. She sent word tae me that Artair was in her care. I sent for him and had him stay at my manor in Dumfries until he was well. We met Diana during our journey north—she was traveling tae visit family in the Highlands. 'Tis not safe for her tae travel alone, so we brought her with us."

Though they'd discussed what they would all tell Laird MacGreghor once they arrived, Liosa's ability to tell the story without blinking an eye impressed Diana.

Laird MacGreghor studied Artair and Liosa for a long moment before giving them a nod.

"'Tis a relief that ye're alive and well. Welcome back, Artair," Laird MacGreghor said, getting to his feet with a smile, and relief swept over Diana. "Ye've no doubt gleaned that yer betrothed is wed tae Niall. Niall told us ye two are kin—'tis why ye bear each other's likeness."

"Aye," Artair said, his eyes straying to Niall and Caitria. "We are. And I'm happy for Caitria and Niall. I can already see 'tis a fine match."

"I'm glad tae hear ye're not angered," Laird MacGreghor said, his smile widening. "Let's get ye all settled in and fed. I'm sure ye're all weary from yer travels. And then I'd like tae have a moment with ye, Artair."

A maid approached and led them out the great hall and up to their guest chambers. As they walked, Diana took in the castle, trying not to gape. The castles in her time were all relics. It was odd— yet exhilarating—to walk through a living, breathing castle, with its high-arched ceilings and tapestries, the bustle of servants moving to and fro, the succulent scent of roasted meats wafting from the kitchens.

The chamber the maid led Diana to was massive, with a four-poster bed and a fireplace that already crackled with a fire. Not long after the maid left her alone, Artair and the others, including Niall and Caitria, filed in.

"Now that we're alone, we have much tae discuss," Artair said. "Diana, can you perform a Silencing spell? We cannae risk being overheard."

She nodded and turned to the door, murmuring the words of the spell.

"*Cuir sileadh an t-seòmair seo bho chluasan daonna.*"

When she turned back around, Niall and Caitria were staring at her with wide eyes.

"You're a stiuireadh?" Niall breathed.

"Yes," she said. "My Aunt Kensa is another stiuireadh—she's the one who influenced your dreams with magic to get you to go back in time to Caitria. She believes that since you traveled back in time without a stiuireadh, something went awry, and Artair was sent to your time."

"She's the one who made me dream of Caitria?" Niall asked, shaking his head in amazement. "Well, I can't be angry with her," he continued. His gaze shifted to Caitria, and he reached for her hand, lifting it to his lips. "I would have never found my wife if I hadn't been drawn to this time."

"I meant what I said in the great hall," Artair said. "I'm happy for ye both. I think Caitria kens that a marriage between us would have been a mistake."

"Aye," Caitria agreed. "But I was worried about ye—we've been searching every part of the Highlands for ye. Latharn has taken up much of the search." Her gaze strayed to Liosa. "Had we kent ye had a sister sooner—"

"It was my foolishness and pride that caused me tae never mention Liosa," Artair said, his voice heavy with regret as he glanced at his sister. "I'm sorry for causing undue worry. Where is Latharn?"

"At yer manor. Father sent a messenger letting him ken ye're here—and alive," Caitria said. "We're glad ye came, but why did ye come here first? Why not yer manor?"

Artair told Niall and Caitria about Tamhas and his men.

"My father-in-law will want tae hear about this," Niall said, looking at Caitria, who nodded in agreement. "Keagan, you should come as well."

After the men left, Liosa excused herself, telling Diana and Caitria that she was tired and needed rest after the journey.

"If ye're not weary from yer journey, I'd love tae walk with ye," Caitria said, offering her a warm smile.

Diana returned it, a stab of shame piercing her as she thought of the jealousy she'd felt when they first met. She could tell that Caitria was warm, kind, and only had eyes for her husband. Caitria could give her insight into how Niall had adjusted to this time, though she told herself she'd ask out of curiosity—not for any other reason.

"I'd like that," she replied.

"I DIDNAE WANT TAE BELIEVE Niall when he told me he was from another time," Caitria said, as they strolled around the castle grounds. "But a part of me knew that he was . . . different. Just as I kent deep down that he wasnae Artair."

Caitria stopped suddenly, turning to face Diana.

"I want ye tae ken—I have no feelings toward Artair other than friendship. My heart belongs only tae Niall."

Diana's face flamed and she lowered her eyes.

"I can tell," she said, giving her a warm smile. "But—it wouldn't be my concern if you did. We're not together."

"Aye?" Caitria asked. "Does Artair ken that? He looks at ye as if ye're the only lass in the world."

Diana swallowed, uncertain if she wanted to reveal that she and Artair were lovers—for the time being. And though she already liked Caitria, she didn't want to discuss her true feelings for Artair.

"You know I'm not from this time. I've only lingered to help him in the fight against Tamhas."

"Niall also isn't from this time," Caitria pointed out. "And he's adjusted quite well."

"Has he?"

"Aye. He serves as the clan historian. When we're not traveling, he's holed up in the library of our manor, reading the manuscripts he's collected or scribbling down notes. I've asked him if he misses the conveniences of the future. He told me he misses hot showers sometimes, but none of that compares tae a life without me."

Caitria's face warmed at this, and Diana felt a pang of envy. If only Artair would express such sentiments to her.

"What would you have done?" Diana asked. "If Niall had chosen to leave?"

Caitria paled, pain flitting across her face.

"My heart would have never healed," she said finally. "I never would have found the love we now share, I'm certain of it. We were meant tae be. I ken it with every part of my body."

Diana's chest tightened as her thoughts strayed to Artair.

"Are ye all right?" Caitria asked, taking in her stormy expression.

"I'm fine," Diana said with forced brightness. "I love this castle—in my time they're mostly relics. Tell me more about it."

She succeeded in changing the subject as Caitria happily obliged.

Diana's thoughts wandered as Caitria spoke, returning to her earlier words. *My heart would have never healed.*

Did her future hold nothing for her but heartbreak, with the chasm of time separating her from the man she loved?

CHAPTER 23

*D*rostan stood with his back to Artair, gazing out the window of his private study.

Artair and Keagan had spent the past hour telling him about Tamhas and the border men's attacks, how Tamhas had followed them north, and their need for men.

Now, Artair regarded him, tension roiling through him. Drostan had not spoken for several long moments. Artair could only assume he was going to refuse offering his assistance.

Artair's chest clenched, and he briefly closed his eyes. Now that Niall was married to his daughter, Artair wasn't part of Clan MacGreghor. Drostan wasn't obligated to help him.

"I ken I'm no longer affiliated with yer clan," Artair said, breaking the long silence. "I—understand if ye cannae help us."

"Ah, ye shame me, Artair," Drostan said,

turning back around to face him with a frown. "Ye've not given me time tae answer."

"I assumed—"

"I was going tae tell ye that though yer sister's lands may not be my lands, that these border men may be far away, I donnae take kindly tae men who bring harm tae innocent people—especially common folk who arenae fighters. And now that he's pursued ye here tae the Highlands," Drostan continued, giving him a smile edged with danger. "The Highlands belong tae the clans. If he comes tae my lands, or tae yers, as ye still remain my ally—this becomes a fight for the MacGreghors."

Relief swelled within Artair and his tension ebbed. Drostan's honor had been one of the main reasons he'd wanted to marry into his family, his clan. He reminded him of his own father's sense of honor, though Drostan wasn't as closed off as his father had been.

"I thank ye," Keagan spoke up. "Laird MacGreghor, for ye tae help people ye're not affiliated with—"

But Drostan interrupted him with a wave of his hand. "Yer brother-in-law remains my ally, and he's a good man. 'Tis why I was going tae marry him tae my daughter, till this imposter came along and stole her heart," he said, giving Niall a teasing smile.

Niall returned his smile, holding his hands up in a mock gesture of guilt.

"I can get fifty tae one hundred men willing tae fight at a moment's notice—perhaps more," Drostan continued, his expression turning serious. "Do ye have men of yer own?"

"I plan tae return tae my manor tomorrow and ask the local men who are willing tae fight tae join me," he said. "Ye should ken—Tamhas may seek men from rival clans tae help."

Drostan's smile was dangerous.

"Then that will give my men even more motivation tae fight. What is yer plan for battle?"

"I want tae lure Tamhas tae my manor," Artair said. "'Tis better if I choose the place where we fight."

"That's wise," Drostan agreed. "I'll send out messengers far and wide tae other clans—foe and ally alike—alerting them that ye've returned tae yer manor. If Tamhas is in the Highlands, he'll soon ken of yer whereabouts. Ye can have the men willing tae fight set up camp on the lands around yer manor. They'll be ready for an attack."

The castle's steward entered with a records book, and Drostan gave them an apologetic smile.

"A laird's duty is never done," he said. "I'll see ye all at supper."

"I'm going tae tell Liosa we have Laird MacGreghor on our side," Keagan said, as they left Drostan's study, hurrying down the corridor and leaving Niall and Artair alone.

Artair gave Niall a sidelong glance as they walked. It was odd to look at the man. Though there were subtle differences between them, looking at him was like gazing into a mirror.

"I know," Niall said, meeting his gaze with a wry smile as if reading Artair's thoughts. "It's strange to me as well."

Artair stopped, studying him with curiosity.

"Ye said we're kin?"

"Yes. I did some digging, and we're related through a distant cousin on your father's side," Niall said. He paused, looking around at the servants who passed, many of whom looked at them with open curiosity. He gestured for Artair to follow him into an empty chamber.

"You should know—I never intended to pose as you. As soon as I arrived here, people just assumed I was you. I was so desperate to help Caitria that I went along with it."

"I bear ye no ill will," Artair said. "What danger was Caitria in?"

Artair listened as Niall told him how a clan noble, Ferghas, had killed Caitria's brother and nearly killed Drostan had he not stopped him.

"I kent Ferghas, and I never trusted him," Artair grumbled. "I'm glad ye stopped the bastard."

"As am I," Niall said. "If I hadn't come to this time . . . "

His eyes darkened, and he shook his head as if shaking the thought away before continuing. "It sounds like you've also had an adventure. I've heard much about stiuireadh—but I've never met one. I assumed there would be something . . . other-worldly about them. Diana seems like a normal woman—a very beautiful one, but—"

Artair didn't realize that his eyes had darkened at the compliment until Niall held up his hands with a chuckle.

"It was just a compliment. I'm happily married, remember?"

Artair gave him a gruff nod. Niall studied him for a long moment before his face broke out in a smile.

"Maybe it's because we share a likeness—but I know that look. You're in love with Diana, aren't you?" he asked.

Artair opened his mouth to deny this, but the words wouldn't come. He stilled, his heart picking up its pace as the realization struck him.

He loved Diana. How could he have been foolish enough to not realize the depth of his feelings for his golden witch? Had he not craved her since he'd first met her—her kindness, her power, her beauty? Would he not burn the world down to protect her? Did the thought of her returning to her own time not cause his heart to splinter? Had she not consumed his thoughts every day and every night?

Now he realized that he'd avoided love for his entire life after watching his father's emotional withdrawal after his mother's death. His father had been a jovial, well-liked man until she died—her death had destroyed him. When Artair took on the lairdship, he didn't want to risk that same vulnerability, that same weakness. That was why he'd been content with marrying

Caitria—while he cared for her, he didn't love or desire her.

But he did love Diana. He loved her to the marrow of his bones. And it took his look-alike, time-traveling relative to tell him what he already knew in his heart.

His emotions must have played out on his face, because Niall gave him an empathetic smile.

"Because we're family, I feel like I have the right to say this," Niall said. "But don't hide your love for her. I still regret waiting to tell Caitria I loved her until I was nearly exiled. I should have told her the moment I realized it. Our type of love —love that's transcended time? It should never be hidden."

~

DIANA WAS as quiet as he was at supper in the great hall that evening, her gaze trained on her meal of roasted lamb and vegetables. He watched her out of the corner of his eye, a tumult of emotions swirling through him, Niall's words echoing in his mind. *Our type of love—love that's transcended time? It should never be hidden.*

How could he tell her how he felt? How could he burden her with the depth of his emotions when she didn't belong in this time? He knew she cared for him—she'd saved his life after all—and she desired him. But to love him, to love him enough to leave her life in the future behind and remain in

this time with him, a time fraught
How could he ask that of her, even i
what he wanted, more than he'd e
anything.

Even with his storm of conflicting emotions, he tried to keep a jovial smile pinned to his face. The other guests in the great hall kept casting glances his way. Word had spread that he'd returned, and the other guests in the hall were looking for signs of jealousy or anger from him over Niall and Caitria's marriage.

He sat at a table with Niall, Caitria, Liosa and Keagan, all of whom were engaged in animated chatter compared to Diana and Artair's relative silence. At times, he felt their curious gazes on him and Diana, yet they didn't press them to join their discussion.

When Niall and Caitria got up from the table to mingle with the other guests, Liosa turned to Artair and Diana. She shared a look with Keagan, who gave her a subtle nod.

"What is it?" Artair asked, his back stiffening with alarm.

"Always prepared for the worst, brother," Liosa said with a teasing smile. "There's nothing tae worry yerself over. 'Tis happy news." She paused, expelling a breath, her smile widening. She looked as if she was about to burst with joy. "I'm with child. 'Tis early days yet, but I've missed my bleeding and the castle healer confirmed it."

"Liosa," he whispered. He reached across the

ᵤe to grip her hand, tears stinging his eyes. His sister was loving and fiercely protective; she would make a wonderful mother. But he couldn't find the words to express his happiness for her.

"I ken, brother," Liosa said, blinking back tears of her own. "I ken."

"Liosa," Diana murmured, beaming. "I'm so happy for you."

"Thank ye, sister," Liosa said. She froze as she realized what she'd said. "I'm sorry, I—"

"It's fine," Diana interjected. "We've spent so much time together since Dumfries it does feel like we're sisters."

Artair's heart clenched; he desperately wanted Liosa's words to be true. Diana as a part of his family, his life. His love.

The musicians began to play, and Keagan stood with a laugh, smiling down at his wife.

"Let's celebrate with a dance."

Liosa took his hand with a grin. Artair turned to ask Diana to dance as well, but she was already getting to her feet.

"Excuse me," she whispered.

He stilled, noticing that her eyes were wet with tears. She hurried away before he could question her.

He got to his feet and followed her, not caring about the whispers and curious looks of the other guests. He trailed her as she rushed down the corridor and out to the courtyard.

"Diana?" he asked, when they were alone.

She turned to face him, her face awash with tears.

"I can't do this," she whispered.

He froze, hot panic searing his chest as his face drained of color.

"What?"

"How long until you have the men you need to fight Tamhas?" she asked.

"I donnae understand why ye're—"

"How long?" she repeated, her voice trembling.

"Drostan's men are going tae gather at my manor within the next two days tae make camp. If Tamhas doesnae show in a fortnight, we plan tae go south tae take the fight tae him."

Diana nodded, looking away from him.

"Why do ye want tae ken?" he asked. "Diana, please. What's wrong?"

"A fortnight. I can do that," she said, ignoring his question as she thought out loud. "After a fortnight, I'll return to my own time. My magic is stronger now, I don't think I need to go back to Tairseach to travel, so I can just perform a spell. You have the MacGreghor clan to help you now. It's not as important that I stay."

"Ye—ye said ye wanted tae help," he said, trying to speak past the pain that twisted his heart.

"I will help," she whispered. "As much as I can, but if the fight isn't over in a fortnight, I'm going to return to my own time. I don't belong here, Artair. It's—it's time for me to go home."

CHAPTER 24

When Diana hurried to her chamber after leaving Artair, she wiped away her tears, embarrassment rushing through her over her near breakdown.

For the entire day, conflicting emotions had torn through her over her love for him and returning to the future. When Liosa accidentally called her her sister, it was as if a dam had burst inside her as she realized how desperately she wanted that to be true. She wanted to be a part of Artair's life as his wife, and Liosa's sister-in-law. The brief surge of joy that filled her at the thought had taken her by surprise—she knew she couldn't remain stoic.

She hadn't expected Artair to follow her out of the hall, and she tried not to think about the pain on his face when she told him it was time to go home. She'd wanted him to tell her to stay, that he loved her, but he'd only stared at her in frozen silence.

It is time for you to go home, she told herself. *You've done what you've said you would do.* Artair had help from Drostan MacGreghor, and soon he would have the help of his own men. If Tamhas arrived within the next couple of weeks, she would do whatever she could to help fight. But then she would leave—she had to. The longer she remained here with Artair, the harder it would be for her when she returned.

She barely slept that night, her mind consumed with images of Artair's pained face and her longing for him. After she awoke, she was still groggy as she washed and changed into another one of Liosa's borrowed gowns.

She avoided looking at Artair as they bid their farewells to Caitria, Niall and Laird and Lady MacGreghor. Due to her pregnancy, Liosa was going to linger behind at the castle until the conflict with Tamhas was resolved.

Liosa embraced her for a long time, pulling back to murmur in her ear, "Tell my brother how ye feel."

Diana stiffened as she met Liosa's eyes. But she shouldn't have been surprised that Liosa knew how she felt about Artair—she had proven to be perceptive.

Liosa just gave her a kind smile and turned to embrace Keagan farewell.

She considered Liosa's advice as she, Artair and Keagan rode to his manor, which wasn't far from the castle.

I can't tell him how I feel, she decided. *He doesn't feel the same, and I already told him I have to go home.* It was best that she set aside her feelings for the remainder of her time here, as difficult as that would be.

When they approached his sprawling gray stone manor, she saw that a line of his servants stood outside, waiting for him with wide smiles.

Standing in the center of them was a tall, handsome man with dark hair and whiskey-colored eyes, stark relief and joy on his face as he took in Artair. She assumed this was Latharn, Artair's loyal servant who'd led the search for him.

As Diana studied him, something seemed familiar about him, though she was certain she'd never seen him before.

"Artair," Latharn said, striding forward to clamp his hand on his shoulder when they'd all dismounted. "I'm glad tae see ye."

"As am I," Artair replied, giving him a wide smile in return. "I'm sorry tae have caused ye worry —and I thank ye for searching for me."

"We're just glad ye're home and alive," Latharn said.

Artair briefly introduced Keagan and Diana to Latharn before stepping forward to greet and embrace each of his servants. He greeted each servant by name, and they seemed genuinely delighted to see him. She even saw several maids' eyes brim with tears. Artair must have been a kind and generous laird. It made her love him even more.

Artair had a maid lead her to her guest chamber while he, Keagan and Latharn left to talk to the locals about fighting Tamhas.

She decided to turn her thoughts away from Artair by practicing several defensive spells and mentally reviewing the spell she'd need to perform to get her back to her time. For this spell, she'd need a focal point from her time, something that would draw her to it. She tried to focus on aspects of her life in the present that she enjoyed—the manor she was restoring in the Highlands. Her reliable job. Her comfortable London flat. Her aunts—both Kensa and Maggie.

Again, none of these tugged on her heart or filled her with longing. Instead, her mind kept conjuring images of the year she was in—bustling medieval villages and cities. Sunlit-dappled groves and lochs. Expansive glens covered with winter frost. Liosa and Keagan's laughter.

Artair's handsome face, smiling at her. His husky voice in her ear. *My golden witch.*

Frustrated, she took a break and explored the manor. It was elegant and refined—dark, hardwood floors, tapestries draped over the walls, burning fireplaces emanating warmth, candlelight casting the rooms in a soft, homey glow. It was her intention to restore the manor in her own time to something like this, a peaceful refuge from the modern world.

Artair and Keagan soon returned, leading her to the drawing room where they informed her they'd found a couple of dozen local men willing to fight. In addition to these men, Drostan's men would make camp tomorrow in the patch of forest adjacent to his manor.

"Now that Drostan's messengers have spread word that I'm back, I pray that word has reached— or will shortly reach—Tamhas," Artair said.

"I can use a Concealing spell to hide the camp away from any who approach your lands. It'll make your manor look as if it's undefended."

Artair gave her a brusque nod while Keagan's eyes went so wide she thought they would pop out of his head.

"I'm sorry," he said, at her look of amusement. "It'll take time for me tae get used tae what ye can do."

"Ye willnae have tae," Artair replied, not looking at her. "Diana is leaving us in a fortnight."

Diana's stomach twisted at the nonchalance in his tone.

"When 'tis time for battle," Artair continued, still not looking at her, "ye can use yer witchcraft tae defend the manor and the stables. We'll have tae make certain the servants are all inside."

"But—I thought I could help you on the field," Diana said with a frown.

"No. Ye'll use yer witchcraft for defense only. I

want this tae be an honest fight. If we rely only on yer magic, we may not be able tae defend ourselves when ye're gone. And," he added, his eyes glittering with the promise of violence, "I want tae be the one who kills Tamhas with my own hands."

He left the drawing room before she could reply. Keagan, who now seemed to sense the distance between them, gave her a sympathetic smile and thanked her before following him out.

She'd hoped to spend alone time with Artair now that they were at his manor, the way they had when they were at Keagan and Liosa's home, but that evening a maid told her that Artair would dine alone tonight as she brought her meal to her chamber. Diana hid her disappointment behind a polite smile.

Artair's avoidance continued over the next few days. Artair would eat his meals alone or with Keagan and Latharn, while Diana ate alone in her chamber. The men who were to fight would show up at the manor just after first light, and Artair would spend most of his days with them, preparing for battle.

Diana spent her days working on her spells or taking brief walks around the manor, battling the loneliness and heartache that swelled within her. Keagan would sometimes join her to keep her company, for which she was grateful, but it was Artair's presence she longed for.

When she did catch glimpses of Artair, he

would merely give her a polite nod of acknowledgment. She told herself that his distance was a good thing, that it would prepare her for his absence from her life in the future, but that didn't stop pain from twisting her heart.

She was surprised when Artair sought her out in her chamber one afternoon, as she was idly performing an Illumination spell on a candle, lighting it and snuffing it out with only a single command in Gaelic. *Solus.*

She jumped when she felt eyes on her, turning to face him. For a moment, she'd seen a brief flare of longing—and something else she couldn't detect —in his eyes, before it disappeared, and that stoic mask returned.

"I'd like for ye tae perform the Concealing spell on the camp. All the men who are fighting have arrived," he said.

She nodded, trying not to show how much his coldness hurt, and followed him out.

He led her to a patch of forest close to the manor, but far from the curious eyes of his men.

She eyed the vantage point that any approaching rider would have and performed the spell, closing her eyes as she murmured the words.

"Thoir sùil air an raon seo bho shealladh daonna. Cruthaich an raon seo bho shùilean daonna."

As he took her to several spots around the camp, she repeated the process, relishing in the feel of power that coiled within her as she uttered the words of the spell.

When she finished the final spell, she turned to face him, freezing when she noticed the look of raw vulnerability in his eyes.

She swallowed as he took a step toward her.

"Diana—" he whispered, but the shouts of his men interrupted him.

Alarm rippling through her, she whirled to face the shouts. Artair was already dashing out of the clearing, and she had to run to keep up with him.

Once they emerged from the clearing, she halted in her tracks.

A lone rider approached the castle. Artair turned to her, his body rigid with tension.

"Get back tae the manor. Use whatever spell ye need tae make certain that no outsider can get in."

She hesitated, not wanting to leave him, her eyes straying to the approaching rider. She stilled as the rider drew closer—she recognized the rider. It was a woman.

Loirin. Tamhas and Iomhar's sister, the woman who'd allowed them to escape.

Loirin dismounted, halting in her tracks as Artair and several men who'd joined them unsheathed their swords. She paled, holding up her hand to show she meant no harm.

"Ye're Tamhas's sister," Artair snarled.

"Aye," Loirin replied, her voice wavering.

"What do ye want?" Artair demanded. "Why are ye here?"

"I'm here tae warn ye about my brother," Loirin said. "He has reinforcements—men from rival clans of the MacGreghors. He and his men will arrive here at first light."

CHAPTER 25

"*I* never wanted any part of what my brothers have done," Loirin said shakily, warming her hands by the fire.

Loirin now sat in the drawing room of Artair's manor. Artair stood opposite her, along with Diana, Latharn and Keagan. Keagan had been suspicious and wanted Artair to take her as a prisoner, but he'd told him that Loirin was the one who'd helped them escape.

Still, he regarded her with wariness as she continued.

"I kept silent out of fear. My brothers—they've always scared me. My father was worse. After Iomhar was killed . . . I didnae shed any tears. Part of me was relieved. I've—I've heard the screams of the lasses he's tormented over the years," she whispered, her eyes filling with tears.

"Why are ye here?" Artair asked. He was sympathetic to the lass, but a part of him remained suspicious. It seemed too convenient that she'd arrived just as he was preparing his men to fight her brother.

"Tae warn ye," Loirin said, raising desperate eyes to meet his. "My brother made me come tae the Highlands with him; I think he kens I want tae run away. When I heard him talk of what he planned tae do to the women—tae the Sassenach lass and Lady Padarsan, I kent I couldnae keep silent."

Terror coiled through Artair; he had to rein in his panic and remain calm. At his side, both Keagan and Diana went pale.

"I came tae tell ye that he plans tae arrive here at first light tomorrow. He thinks ye're not prepared. He plans tae slaughter ye and all who support ye and take the Sassenach and Lady Padarsan hostage. I—I donnae want tae repeat what he said he intends tae do tae them. But ye need tae prepare yourselves for his arrival."

"Where is he now?" Artair asked, rage clawing through his chest. He couldn't wait to kill the bastard.

"Camped out in a forest just south of here," Loirin replied. "He has over one hundred men. He's promised tae share yer riches with them once he's killed ye."

He studied Loirin, trying to ascertain if she was telling the truth or if this was a trick. But there was genuine fear in her eyes.

"I thank ye for coming here, at great risk tae

yerself," he said, believing her words to be the truth. "If ye want tae stay, I can offer ye protection—"

"No," Loirin said quickly. "I—I cannae stay. He'll come looking for me and ken I've told ye of his plans. 'Tis best if he thinks ye're unprepared. And as much of a monster as my brother has become, I donnae think he'll hurt me."

"Are you certain?" Diana spoke up, her brow furrowed with concern. "We saw you with a baby when we escaped the first time. Is the child—"

"The bairn is safely in Lockerbie with her mother," Loirin interrupted. "She's not mine, just one of Iomhar's many bastards. I felt pity for the child. I willnae have bairns until I've escaped from Tamhas or if he falls in battle," she added, giving Artair a meaningful look. "'Tis only a matter of time. His deeds have made him many enemies."

She left after refusing any more food or drink, and he and Diana stood in front of his manor, watching her vanish into the distance on her horse.

"I wish we'd convinced her to stay," Diana murmured. "Do you think she'll be all right?"

"Aye. She kens her brother better than we do," he said. He turned to face her, his body going tense. "Diana, what she said about Tamhas coming after ye—"

"No," Diana interrupted, giving him a defiant look. "Don't you dare tell me to get myself to safety. I gave you my word that I'd help, and that's what I intend to do. Tamhas can *try* to harm me," she said, darkness entering her eyes. "He doesn't know what I'm capable of."

Artair couldn't help but smile as he gazed into the eyes of the woman he loved. His fierce golden witch. His heart.

"I have tae spend the rest of the day with my men preparing for tomorrow's fight. I—I ken I've been absent—"

"Artair, you don't have to—" she began.

"No," he returned. "I owe ye my apology. I was hurt when ye said ye needed tae go home. I wanted tae try and purge ye from my mind, but that didnae work. It just made me want ye more. I want tae share supper with ye tonight, just the two of us. There's something I want tae discuss with ye."

He was going to tell her how he felt. It had been on the tip of his tongue to tell her earlier, before the shouts of his men and Loirin's approach had interrupted them.

He was tired of hiding his love from her; it wouldn't change how he felt or make her departure any less painful. He would do everything he could to survive tomorrow's battle, but he wanted her to know how he felt before he stepped onto the battle-field. If he fell tomorrow, he could do it knowing that Diana was aware of his love for her.

Turmoil filled her expression; he feared she'd refuse him. But she gave him a brief nod of acquies-cence before turning to head back inside.

For the remainder of the day, he had to force himself to concentrate on his tasks: running drills with his men, riding with Latharn to the nearby village to warn the locals to flee or prepare to defend themselves if Tamhas's men ventured there.

Fatigue had settled in on him by the time he returned to the manor for his private supper with Diana, which his servants had set up in his chamber at his request.

But as soon as he found Diana waiting for him, a vision of loveliness in a gown of forest green, her honey-colored hair loose around her shoulders, his fatigue vanished. He drank in the sight of her, wanting to sear her into his memory.

"Diana," he whispered. "I love ye."

He froze as the words fell past his lips. He'd meant to share supper with her first, to offer her another apology for his distance, and then tell her how he felt. But the words had tumbled from his lips before he could stop them.

He waited, his mouth dry and his heart hammering against his chest as he waited for her response. But she remained silent, her face pale with shock.

"I—I'm sorry," he said, as the silence stretched. "I shouldnae have—"

"Artair," Diana interrupted, her voice wavering. "Shut up."

She crossed to him in three long strides, pressing her lips to his. He fiercely returned her kiss, holding her body close.

"Artair," she whispered, when they broke apart. "I love you too. I killed a man to save your life. I'd do it again, a thousand times over. I love you, Artair Dalaigh. I was a prat to try and fight my feelings for you—"

"No. I was the fool," Artair whispered. "Tae avoid ye for days when I wanted nothing more than tae have ye at my side. Tae try tae deny what my body has always kent."

Their lips met again, and he swung her up into his arms, the meal forgotten. He lowered her gown and bent down to capture one of her rosy nipples in his mouth, suckling eagerly, as she arched against him. She reached down to stroke him, and he sucked in his breath as he lowered her to her feet.

Diana took the lead, stepping out of her gown before undressing him. He sat down on the bed, aching for her as she straddled him, sinking down onto his erect hardness.

They both moaned, and he placed his hands on her buttocks as she began to ride him, throwing her head back and gasping as he leaned forward to lave her breasts with his tongue.

"Diana," he whispered. "My Diana. I love ye."

"And I love you," she returned, making his heart swell with joy. "So very much."

She suddenly arched upright, her eyes rolling back as her orgasm claimed her. His climax followed hers, and he let out a roar of pleasure as his body shook with its force.

Diana slumped forward, out of breath as she rested her head on his shoulder. He kept her in his arms as he rolled back onto the bed.

For several long moments they just lay there in silence, the only sound in the room the crackling of the fire and their quick breaths. Diana finally sat up, reaching out to trace her fingers along his torso.

"Artair," she whispered. "About tomorrow, and after the—"

"No," he silenced her. "I want tae only think about tonight. Now that I ken ye love me, I'll fight even harder."

"Ye're not going tae fall in battle tomorrow, Artair. If I have to kill more men to prevent that from happening, I'll do it," Diana said, her expression turning fierce.

"My love," he murmured, though pride rippled through him at the determination in her tone. "We agreed that tomorrow will be a fair fight—no witchcraft. Ye'll protect the manor and the servants inside."

Conflict filled her eyes, but she didn't protest.

"You come back to me tomorrow, Artair Dalaigh," she whispered.

"I will do everything I can tae return tae ye," he returned. "Diana . . . loving ye has made me realize something about myself. I never wanted tae admit this tae myself before, but I think it was because of my father that I closed myself off for so long."

"Your father?"

"Aye. After my mother died . . . he withdrew from me and Liosa. Her loss destroyed him. I remember thinking that I didnae want love tae destroy me. It was why I was content tae have a loveless marriage with Caitria. Ye've changed everything for me, Diana."

Her eyes filled at his words, and he peppered kisses along her jaw, her throat, and down to her breasts. He wanted to again show her with his body, and his words, how much he loved her. How much he would always love her.

"Hold still, my golden witch," he whispered. "I have days of neglect tae make up for."

"You do," she agreed with a chuckle, but her chuckle soon turned to a low moan of pleasure.

CHAPTER 26

*A*rtair's heart pounded like a battering ram against his ribcage as he stood on the front lines of his men, waiting for Tamhas's men to appear. It was just before first light, and he had to force thoughts of Diana to the back of his mind, knowing they would be a distraction—the firelight illuminating her beautiful body as she rode him, the words of love they'd exchanged.

They'd made love once more before rising long before the servants: Diana to place protective charms and spells around the entrances to the home, Artair to make his way out to the camp. They'd exchanged a long, passionate kiss before parting, and even though he'd done his best to reassure her, Artair had felt the wetness of her tears on his face.

I will kill Tamhas today, he promised himself. *I will end this, and there will be no lingering threat tae Diana or tae my family.*

231

The sound of stampeding horses pulled him to the present, and he stiffened, his hand tightening on the hilt of his sword. He turned to Latharn and Keagan who flanked him. They both gave him nods, indicating they were ready.

Artair turned and gestured for his men to charge.

They darted out from the trees just as Tamhas's men appeared in the distance. Though a fog had settled over the land, he could see the startled expressions of Tamhas's men as he and his men charged forward.

Both sides collided in a blur of metallic sword clashes, grunts, and colliding bodies. Artair's sword clashed with the sword of a large, burly man. They fought, whirling around each other, before he kicked the man to the ground, turning to fight off another man, and then another, his movements rapid.

He'd fought only twice before in his life; both times for the MacGreghor clan. He'd been trained to fight by some of the strongest warriors of the clan. But there was nothing like the true ferocity of battle.

His movements were purely guided by instinct, and as he fought, he searched the fighting bodies for Tamhas, finally locating him in the center of the fighting men, dark glee filling his eyes as he ran a man through with his sword. Artair charged at him with a growl, and Tamhas turned, a fierce rage entering his eyes.

Their swords clashed in midair as they began to fight. Tamhas was a strong fighter, meeting Artair blow by blow. For a while they were evenly matched, but Tamhas soon managed to kick Artair in the abdomen, sending him to his knees. Tamhas knocked him to the ground with the hilt of his sword and stepped forward, his eyes bright with fury as he pressed his foot to Artair's throat.

"Was it ye or yer Sassenach bitch that killed my brother?"

"It was me," Artair rasped, struggling to free himself from Tamhas's hold. "He wept like a lassie when I threw him against the wall. I'd kill him again if I had the chance."

Tamhas let out a roar of rage, lifting his sword to stab him straight through, but someone struck him from behind, giving Artair the opportunity to roll away.

It was Latharn who'd struck Tamhas, and as he fought Tamhas, Artair stumbled to his feet. Together, he and Latharn's swords clashed with Tamhas's, but Tamhas expertly defended himself against the both of them.

Latharn had to turn away from the fight when two other men charged him from behind. Artair poured every ounce of his strength into his sword thrusts as he and Tamhas continued to fight. He needed to hasten their fight before Tamhas exhausted him; he reared back and lunged forward, piercing Tamhas in the abdomen with his sword.

Tamhas howled with pain, one hand lowering

to clutch his bleeding abdomen, all the while continuing to fight Artair with the other.

"I think ye're lying!" Tamhas shouted, his voice wavering with pain and fury over the metallic clangs of their swords. "I think yer whore killed my brother. I will see her dead at the end of my sword —after me and my men have had time tae enjoy her body."

Hot rage surged through him, and Artair lunged forward, determined to deal the final, fatal blow, when another one of Tamhas's men charged at him. Artair had no choice but to whirl around and fight him off, knocking him unconscious with the hilt of his sword.

When he turned back around, panic darted through him when he saw that Tamhas was gone. He stumbled forward, frantic, until he spotted Tamhas racing toward a horse tied up to a nearby tree, still clutching his abdomen. At first, he assumed Tamhas was being a coward and fleeing battle, and then he remembered Tamhas's threat.

Fear sliced through him. Tamhas was going after Diana.

He knew that Diana had put protective spells around his manor, but what if Tamhas still found a way in and caught her off guard?

Artair charged after Tamhas, mounting another horse and racing after him. Artair kept his focus trained on Tamhas, kicking the sides of his horse to make him move faster. He tightened his grip on the reins as his horse closed in on

Tamhas, until they were riding almost side by side.

He reached for his sword and slashed out at Tamhas. Tamhas evaded the blow, but his horse panicked and reared back, tossing Tamhas to the ground.

Artair leapt from his horse, darting toward Tamhas's prone form, raising his sword, but Tamhas stumbled to his feet.

It happened impossibly fast. Tamhas lunged forward, plunging his sword into Artair's abdomen and twisting it, as pain like Artair had never known tore through him.

He sank to his knees, pressing his hands to his bleeding wound, when he heard a scream—a familiar scream—behind him.

Panic careened through his injured body. It was Diana. She was here. *No.*

Tamhas removed his sword from Artair's abdomen, a sickening look of hunger flitting across his face as he looked past him.

"Ye get tae watch while I rape and kill yer whore," Tamhas hissed.

Artair turned as Diana approached them through the wisps of fog, looking like the powerful witch she was, her golden hair wafting around her in the morning breeze. She was all fire and fury as she raised her hands.

"Diana—no," he managed to rasp.

She stopped, her face still white with fury, as he stumbled to his feet, hissing in pain at the effort.

Tamhas was striding toward Diana, and though he clutched his abdomen and his face was going pale with blood loss, a dark, eager look filled his expression.

Artair met Diana's eyes. She gave him a small nod, seeming to know what he was thinking as he charged toward Tamhas from behind, using his preoccupation with Diana to his benefit.

He's my kill.

"Tamhas!" Artair shouted, because even though Tamhas was a bastard, Artair's honor wouldn't allow him to stab him in the back.

Tamhas turned, lifting his sword to strike, but Artair used his remaining strength to lunge forward, plunging his sword into Tamhas's heart.

He took dark pleasure in the way Tamhas's eyes widened in surprise, how he sank to his knees as his blood spread across his chest.

"My Diana did kill yer rapist of a brother," Artair rasped, fighting past his growing weakness and pain to speak. "And it was yer sister who alerted us tae yer presence. She kens what a monster ye've become. Now ye cannae harm anyone else."

He saw one last trace of defiance in Tamhas's eyes, one last flare of rage, before his eyes fluttered shut, and he slumped to the ground, lifeless.

Only then did Artair succumb to his own injury, stumbling to his knees. With a strangled sob, Diana rushed to him, pulling him into his arms.

"Artair," she gasped. "Hold still. I'm going to get you help."

He fought to find words, to tell her how much he loved her, but his pain swelled, and her lovely, grief-stricken face dissolved to blackness.

CHAPTER 27

*F*or the next several days, Diana remained at Artair's side, gripping his hand, her emotions ranging from relief to anxiety.

During the battle, she had sensed that something was wrong, that her Artair was in fatal danger —maybe it was her magic, maybe it was pure instinct. She'd left the manor, mounting a horse as she murmured the words of a Locator spell. *Seall dhomh Artair Dalaigh.*

The spell led her to the sound of swords clashing in the heavy fog that bathed the land—to Artair and Tamhas.

Latharn and Keagan had found her in the glen with Artair after he'd slipped from consciousness; they'd carried him back to the manor and sent for a local healer. The healer had successfully stopped his bleeding and cleaned the wound, binding it securely. When the healer told them that Artair would recover, Keagan had reached out to steady Diana as she swayed on her feet with relief.

"But he'll need much rest before he's fully recovered. Make certain he imbibes hot broth and apply honey or wine to the wound as it heals," the healer told them, before leaving.

Diana hadn't left his side, feeding him herself and cleaning his wound whenever he drifted to consciousness, murmuring words of the two Healing spells she knew.

She'd told him what happened in the battle's aftermath during his moments of consciousness. His men had soundly defeated Tamhas's men, who were taken by surprise at the number of men who'd come to Artair's aid. Not long after Tamhas's death, his men had surrendered on the battlefield. Laird MacGreghor had sent Tamhas's men back to the border with a message of warning: anyone who retaliated or continued to harm and steal from the locals would suffer the wrath of the MacGreghor clan.

Artair had given her a smile after she'd informed him of this, relief flitting across his pale, handsome features before he drifted back to sleep.

Drostan MacGreghor, his wife Liusaidh, Niall, Caitria, Liosa, and Keagan had all visited Artair during his days of drifting in and out of consciousness. Niall had supplied Artair with penicillin that he'd smuggled from the twenty-first century; Diana had nearly kissed him in gratitude.

Liosa stayed at his side almost as long as she

did, and Keagan had to constantly remind her to take breaks and rest for the sake of their unborn child.

"Do ye think I was harsh with him? When ye both first arrived and I slapped him?" Liosa asked Diana one evening as they both sat at Artair's side. Tears brimmed in her eyes as she studied the pale face of her brother.

"No," Diana said firmly, reaching out to give her hand a reassuring squeeze. "I think you were upset, and he understood why."

"I'm not letting him slip from my life again. He's going tae be a part of my child's life as his uncle," Liosa said fiercely.

"Artair's not going anywhere," Diana said, smiling. "He loves you so much. That's why he fought Tamhas and his men."

"Donnae flatter my sister, Diana," Artair rasped, his eyes fluttering open as he gave them both a weak smile. "She'll never forget a compliment and use it against ye."

Liosa laughed, looking relieved that Artair was awake, and leaned forward to embrace him.

Diana watched, beaming, as Liosa and Artair traded good-natured barbs. Artair was still pale, but he looked well on the way to a full recovery.

After a full week had passed, Artair was getting impatient with his confinement, so they began to take walks around the manor for him to regain his strength.

As they walked, he would tell her more about

his years growing up at the manor, pointing out the places where he and Liosa would play as children, and which exits he'd used to sneak out of to go riding or hunting with friends.

But Artair never asked her about her intentions of staying—or leaving this time. She realized that she was waiting for him to ask her to stay, because she already knew what her answer would be. She'd had a lot of time to think while sitting at his bedside as he drifted, and she knew that her life in the future would be an empty shell without Artair. She wanted to stay here, to make a life with him.

But as the week wore on with Artair never bringing up the matter, her hope of him asking her to stay had begun to ebb.

At the end of the second week of his recovery, he came to fetch her from her chamber. She looked up at him in surprise. It relieved her to see him looking handsome and healthy.

But as she met his eyes, she noticed that he looked nervous.

"Artair?" she asked. "What is it?"

"Will ye take a ride with me? And before ye ask, I've already spoken tae the healer. I'm well enough tae ride."

She gave him a nod, still puzzled over his obvious nervousness. When they mounted his horse, he didn't tell her where they were going.

"Ye'll ken when ye see it," he said cryptically, as they rode away from the manor and into the surrounding countryside.

She looked around. There was something familiar about her surroundings, something she couldn't quite pinpoint. But as they approached a looming manor in the distance, her heart leapt into her throat.

The manor was the same crumbling family manor she was restoring in her own time. In this time, it was smaller and hadn't yet fallen into disrepair, its stone exterior intact and gleaming in the sun.

Artair slowed down the horse to a trot, dismounting and helping her down. She shook her head in amazement as he tied up his horse.

"How did you find it?" she asked in disbelief.

"I remembered something yer aunt told me in yer time. When I showed her where my manor was on a map, she told me it wasnae far from the manor ye were restoring. I kent it wasnae likely, but I had Latharn and some of my men do a search for unoccupied manors in the same area as yer manor while I was recovering in my chamber. Latharn found it and described it tae me. It was a risk, and I kent I could have been wrong, but it sounded like yer family's manor. Latharn located the owner of the lands— he resided in Inverness and was on the verge of renting the lands. I suspect he's an ancestor of yers. We're still working out the details, but I purchased the land from him—and that includes the manor."

Diana shook her head, overwhelmed at the

steps Artair had taken to obtain the manor—all while he was recuperating.

She looked back at the manor, her mind still reeling. She knew her family's home had fallen into periods of disuse, during which times they'd still owned the lands: this time period was one of them.

"Artair, this is amazing," she whispered. "But . . . I don't understand. Why did you purchase it?"

Artair didn't answer. Instead, he lowered himself to one knee. The world tilted around her as Artair gave her a sheepish smile.

"Niall told me this is how men propose in yer time," he said. "Am I doing it right?"

Diana smiled as her eyes filled, her heart picking up its pace.

"Yes," she whispered. "You're doing it right."

He took a breath, then reached for her hand.

"I love ye, Diana. My fierce, golden witch. My heart. I want tae build a home with ye—here. A life with ye. I want ye tae be my wife. My lady. My family. Will ye stay with me in this time, my love? Will ye marry me?"

Her heart swelled at the open look of vulnerability—and love—in his eyes.

"Yes, Artair," she whispered. "I'll marry you. I want to be yours. Always."

Artair stood, swinging her up in his arms as he kissed her. She returned his kiss, joy flooding her body in a dizzying rush.

It struck her then that this was the reason she'd always felt such a pull toward the manor in her time. It was why it always filled her with a sense of . . . home. Because it would one day be her home, only in another time. Her home with the man she loved.

~

THAT EVENING, as Diana got dressed for a celebratory dinner with Artair and the others, she froze when she saw her aunt appear like an apparition on the edge of the manor grounds.

Diana smiled, glad that the Summoning spell she'd performed earlier had worked.

She tugged on a cloak and hurried outside, approaching her waiting aunt. Kensa stood with her back to her, her long, dark hair whipping around her in the wind.

When Diana reached her side, she could see that Kensa looked considerably younger than her actual age of forty-seven; she looked to be in her mid-twenties. It was a side effect of her abilities, something that only happened to a small percentage of stiuireadh—the appearance of rapid aging and de-aging whenever she traveled through time or performed one of her more powerful spells. Diana had only seen such an effect on two other stiuireadh when she was younger, and even though she knew the cause, it was always startling to see.

Pushing aside her slight surprise, Diana linked her arms with Kensa's.

"Did you know that I would fall in love with

Artair?" Diana asked, by way of greeting. "Artair's purchasing our family's ancestral manor—which you told him about."

"I told him about the manor. But only as an observation. Believe it or not, I didn't intend for you two to end up together," Kensa said with a wry chuckle. "But . . . I did notice the attraction between you two back at my cottage. I didn't need magic to see that. It wasn't me that purposefully brought you two together. That was the two of you on your own. Or just . . . fate." She turned, giving Diana a wide smile. "I'm so happy for you, niece. Artair is a good man."

Diana beamed, resting her head on Kensa's shoulder.

"Will you tell Aunt Maggie? And handle things in London for me?"

"Of course," Kensa said. "Your aunt will be annoyed. We both know she's not a fan of magic or time travel. But I think she'll understand."

"Kensa . . . I want to apologize," Diana said in a rush, lifting her head from Kensa's shoulder. "For avoiding you after my parents died. For pushing you away. Magic was so entwined with my grief . . . it wasn't until I embraced my magic that I let go of that pain."

"There's nothing to apologize for," Kensa reassured her. "Your path has led you right here where you belong. What do you plan to do in this time?"

"I think I can use my law background to help Artair manage the manor's property records and taxes, along with the tenants. And," she added tentatively, "I'm thinking of helping other travelers if I can. Ones who arrive in this time. I have magic . . . I might as well use it to help."

Kensa widened her eyes, looking pleasantly surprised.

"Oh, Diana," she said. "That would be wonderful. I can visit you from time to time and assist you."

"I'd like that," Diana said. "I'm wondering if I already have some of the same instincts that you do. When I met Artair's close servant and friend, Latharn, something struck me about him. Something familiar."

"Ah," Kensa said, nodding with understanding. "That was your magic reacting to someone else who will soon be affected by time travel. It could mean he will travel himself, or he'll become involved with another traveler."

"Do I have to do anything?"

"No. You would know if you did. I often have visions of those I'm meant to help: I see them in my dreams or in my Conjuring spells. Whoever will affect this Latharn, she's likely already on her way here. And I suspect it may indeed be a 'she.'"

They stood in companionable silence for a moment as Diana considered her words, wondering about the identity of this mysterious traveler was who would enter Latharn's life.

The sound of an approaching horse pulled her from her thoughts. She turned as she saw Niall and Caitria approach the manor on horseback. Artair had sent for them so they could join their celebratory dinner, along with Liosa and Keagan.

Liosa and Keagan had been delighted over the news of their engagement. Artair told her that they were going to move into Artair's manor after he and Diana moved into her family's ancestral home. Liosa and Artair wanted to remain close together after so many years of separation. They were having a trusted steward handle the transfer of their manor to one of Keagan's relatives.

"I should head back inside," Diana said, glancing back at her aunt. "Do you want to join us?"

"No, I need to return," Kensa said. "But summon me for your wedding. I want to see my niece get married."

"I will," Diana promised. She moved forward to embrace her aunt, who held her tight before pecking her on the cheek.

"Now get back inside," Kensa said. "Your handsome Highlander is waiting for you."

Diana gave Kensa's hand one last squeeze, turning to make her way back to the manor.

When she glanced behind her, Kensa had vanished.

Diana entered the manor, finding the others gathered in the dining room. Artair strode toward her with a loving smile.

"I was wondering where ye were," he said.

"Just saying goodbye to someone," she said. At

his confused frown, she added, "Kensa. I summoned her."

"Ah," he said. "I hope ye thanked her for bringing us together."

"My aunt, the time-traveling matchmaker, didn't know we would end up together," she said with a chuckle. "We did that all on our own."

"Aye. We did," he murmured, pulling her close for a brief but searing kiss.

"Brother, can ye at least wait for the wedding tae kiss and moon about yer bride?" Liosa asked, with an exaggerated groan.

Artair laughed, keeping his eyes trained on Diana.

"I cannae help myself, sister," he said. He lowered his voice, his next words for her ears only, making her heart fill with joy. "I love ye, my golden witch. Always."

And, ignoring the mock groans of Liosa and the others, he pulled her in for another searing kiss.

CHAPTER 28

L atharn watched from the rear of the great
hall of MacGreghor Castle as Diana and
Artair sealed their wedding vows with a
kiss. Everyone in the great hall cheered as they
broke apart, flushed and smiling, as Drostan
MacGreghor ordered everyone to feast and make
merry.

Latharn smiled, watching as the guests
swarmed Artair and Diana to offer their congratulations. He wished he could stay and enjoy the
wedding festivities. It was good to see Artair so
happy. But Latharn needed to leave the celebration
early; he had a long journey to make.

During Artair's long absence, he'd learned
something that shook his entire world.

The family he'd always known, who loved him
and he loved in return, whom he'd worked as a
servant to help support, wasn't his true family. He
was the son and heir of the chieftain and Laird

Seoras MacUisdein, whose brother had murdered him and took leadership of his clan, and his castle, for himself. His uncle had then murdered his two brothers, but his mother had smuggled Latharn out of the MacUisdein lands when he was still a babe, sending him off to live with a loyal servant, Cahir, on distant lands.

He was only supposed to live with them temporarily, but after his birth mother died while under imprisonment, Cahir had raised him as his own. He'd gone his entire life thinking he was a man of humble birth. He'd secretly longed for more, but contented himself serving as Artair's most trusted and loyal servant.

Perhaps he would have persisted in his ignorance had it not been for his mother's deathbed confession. His father—the man he'd thought was his father—had died of illness several years ago. She'd told him everything, begging him for forgiveness, telling him they'd only withheld the truth from him to protect him. They loved him like he was their own, and if his uncle knew he was still alive, he'd send men to kill him.

She was telling him now because she'd learned that his uncle had recently died, and there was a dispute over who would assume leadership of the clan.

At first, he'd been furious with his parents for withholding such a secret, until he considered the sacrifice they'd made. Had his uncle discovered they were hiding him, they—and his entire family—

would have been killed. He'd thanked his mother, told her he loved her and forgave her.

And he knew what he had to do.

He'd only lingered behind to help Artair with Tamhas and his men to perform his final duty as his servant. He'd told Artair what he'd learned a fortnight ago, that he would be leaving his service to claim his birthright. His mother had told him that there were still men loyal to his slain parents, who had never considered his uncle a legitimate leader; they would follow Latharn if he returned.

"I always kent there was something more tae ye," Artair had told him, clamping his hand on his shoulder. "Ye're a good man, and ye've served me well. If ye need anything from me, I'm always here."

Latharn's heart warmed at the memory of Artair's words as he stepped forward, joining the throng of well-wishers. He reached Diana first, giving her a respectful bow, but she waved it off and reached out to embrace him.

"I think you'll find happiness of your own with a bonnie lass," she said when she released him, probing his eyes with her own. "And sooner than you think."

He studied her with a baffled frown. During the past few weeks, he'd caught her staring at him a few times. He wondered now if this was what those looks were about.

But he doubted this was true. He had a fight ahead of him to claim his place as laird and chieftain of his clan. He had no time to court or marry a lass. Once he claimed his lairdship, he'd marry a suitable lass, likely one of noble birth, who would help cement his claim and give him sons to carry on his line.

He merely gave Diana a polite smile before offering Artair his congratulations—and a farewell.

"Donnae forget—if ye need anything, send a messenger or a letter. I'll help ye if I can."

"I thank ye," Latharn said, holding the gaze of the man he'd served and admired for so long, before turning to head out of the festive bustle of the great hall.

He headed out to the courtyard where a stable boy brought him his horse, already loaded with a bag of supplies for his journey.

Latharn mounted his horse and cast one last look at the castle before riding out of the courtyard. His days of serving others had come to an end. Now was the time to embrace his destiny as a leader.

He rode out of the castle gates, ready to claim his birthright—and his future.

READ LATHARN's *Destiny* (*Highlander Fate Book Six*) *now.*

ABOUT THE AUTHOR

Stella Knight writes time travel romance and historical romance novels. She enjoys transporting readers to different times and places with vivid, nuanced heroes and heroines.

She resides in sunny southern California with her own swoon-worthy hero and her collection of too many books and board games. She's been writing for as long as she can remember, and when not writing, she can be found traveling to new locales, diving into a new book, or watching her favorite film or documentary. She loves romance, history, mystery, and adventure, all of which you'll find in her books.

Stay in touch! Visit Stella Knight's website to join her newsletter.

Stay in touch!
stellaknightbooks.com

Made in the USA
Monee, IL
17 April 2023

32008788R00152